THE WAY TO A KILLER'S HEART 3

NEICY P.

The Way to A Killer's Heart 3

Copyright © 2017 Neicy P.

Published By: Shan Presents

www.shanpresents.com

All rights reserved.

This book is a work of fiction. Names, characters, places, and incidents either are the product of the author's imagination or are used fictitiously and are not to be construed as real. Any resemblance to actual persons, living or dead, business establishments, events, or locales, is entirely coincidental.

No part of this book may be used or reproduced in any manner whatsoever without the prior written consent of the publisher and author, except in the case of brief quotations embodied in critical articles and reviews.

SUBSCRIBE

Text Shan to 22828 to stay up to date with new releases, sneak peeks, contest, and more...

WANT TO BE A PART OF SHAN PRESENTS?

To submit your manuscript to Shan Presents, please send the first three chapters and synopsis to submissions@shanpresents.com

PROLOGUE
EIGHT YEARS AGO

Jason

"What do you see Sin?" I asked in a whisper. We were on the coast of Mexico trying to take out the drug cartel that also had been trafficking women and children. It wasn't something that we usually did, but some of the little girls were being sold to two of the US Senators. When the U.S. Senators didn't want to pay them, Nicholas Domingo sent someone out there to kill them. The shit was fucked up all the way around. We were out here to retaliate for some children raping muthafuckers. No one was worrying about the kids, until Nicholas post the deaths of the Senators online. Dexter was able to take it of the web, but it already had up to a million views.

Dexter also pulled up the pictures and videos off a secret site that Nicholas had for the buyers. Six more seal teams were sent to the other buyers to bring them in. They were going to face felony charges. We had orders to go after the head nigga in charge. It was eleven of us in the group. Matthews, Tags, Geronimo, and Rocs were with Flex, their Squad leader. Sincere, Juda, Dragon, and Stipes were with me. Dexter was in a van near the house that our target was in.

He kept us all connected and had somehow gotten into their security system. He had access to all of their security cameras on the inside. We already knew how many people were in there and which doors were going to lead us to the women and children. We were in the front on top of a hill. Flex's team was in the back. It wouldn't take shit for us to bust through the front gate. Juda already set the bombs there where they also had a small house that held eight guards. It was sitting ten feet from the gate.

It was a two-story house with six balconies. It also had a rooftop deck with a bar and a pool. There was an iron gate that circled around the property. Guards were all around the area. We were told to bring them in alive. By the way those kids were looking, they better hoped that we killed them quick. Because alive is what them muthafuckers weren't going to be after we left that bitch.

"I see some movement on the west side. EM2 is set up and ready to move in on word." Sin answered.

"Dex, tell me what you see on the inside?" I asked on the com.

"There's four of them at the front entrance and six in the back. There are three of them guarding the survivors." He answered.

"What's up with the movement on the west, EM2?" I asked.

"Nothing is going on. We just waiting on the word, Davis." Flex answered.

"Stay alert, EM2." I told him. Flex's team was always ready to get into shit without thinking it through. I tried to switch some things around but it was the same outcome. Judah was with his team before. He asked to switch off to my squad because he didn't connect with them. He said that Matthews gave off a bad vibe.

Matthews got moved around a lot. He got into fights with his teams while they were on missions and shit. They wanted to give him another chance and teamed him up with other crazy muthafuckers. We all had a story on why we weren't right. Even Dexter was fucked up in a way. Matthews was batshit crazy, though. I heard some stories about him and seen the shit he did. But overall, he didn't do anything to warn us of his behavior. He has been working with us for almost two years now with no issues.

"What's the word again?" Flex asked.

"Stop your shit and wait for the word." I answered. We had to make sure that the main guy was there before we went in. Once Dex gave us the ok, we were going in quietly and catching all those muthafuckers sleeping. I didn't want us to be loud if we didn't have to be. So, we waited. And waited. I had a bad feeling about this meeting. Something was off and I couldn't put my finger on it. This was one of the simplest missions that we ever been on. Sincere looked at me and knew that something was wrong.

"The feeling." Sin asked.

"Yeah. I been feeling this shit since we got the orders." I responded.

"Let's hope that you're wrong this time." Sin turned and looked at me. "They call it a Royale with cheese." He said.

"*Pulp Fiction*," I answered. When we waited like this, we played movie or music trivia. He shared one of my favorites with Pops. His ass watched movies all day long with his sister.

"I don't want to survive. I want to live." I told him.

"Nigga, now you know that was my shit. *12 Years a Slave*. But I got one for that ass, though. *I mean, funny like I'm a clown? I amuse you?*" He said. I stared forward. I knew it had to be a movie that I hadn't seen in a long time ago, but it had to been a classic. Sin started smiling like he had me. I shook my head and let him think that.

POW! POW! POW!

Sin picked up his binoculars and looked through them. "Talk to me Flex. What do you see, Sin?" I asked. I didn't get nothing but static from the coms.

"I don't see them. They are not in position." Sin said.

I pressed the com and called out to Dexter. "What do you see on the inside, Dex?"

"Tags and the others are running through, but I don't see Flex. Get in there." Dex yelled.

"Fuck! Move out!" I told my gang.

Juda pressed the detonator and the front gate blew up with smoke screening the area. We went through the smoke shooting off the enemies that weren't dead. We made it through the front door and heard the shots upstairs.

"Flex, check in." I said. More static came through the headset. I motioned for Juda and Dragon to go upstairs, while Sincere and I continued on the first floor with Stipes. We crept through the house with our guns up and ready to shoot. I walked over three bodies to get to a closed door.

"There are four guys behind that door." Dex said.

"How are they lined up?" I asked.

"One on each side of the door. One is standing in the middle of the room and there is one that is standing by the window on the left side. I am measuring up the angles now." He said and started typing. Sincere walked over to the left side of the house with his MK16 SCAR pointed at the wall. "They are three feet from each other by the door. The one by the window is eight feet away from the guy in the middle." I placed my MK16 on my back and pulled out my SIG Sauer P226. I placed my gun on one side of the door and Stipes placed his on the other. We let off our shots with a nod of my head. Dexter confirmed that our targets were down.

"ET1," Dragon came through.

"Go ahead," I answered.

"We found EM2. DOA." Dragon said.

"Are any of our guys up there?" I asked. I couldn't believe that Flex was gone.

"No ET1. Nicholas Domingo is not up here. We went through every room." He answered. We heard shots coming from downstairs and turned.

"We hear shots in the basement. Meet us at the stairs." I told them. We moved swiftly through the house, looking for the rest of the team. We followed the shots with our guns raised. We went back into the front entrance and walked down a set of stairs that led to the basement. We heard yelling and screaming. "Sound off!" I yelled.

"Petty Officer Duke," I heard Tags say.

"Petty Officer Green," Geronimo said after him.

Rocs responded with Petty Officer Lewis. I waited to hear

Matthews. I turned the corner and saw Matthews gutting one of the enemies like a fish. He had blood all over his face and uniform. The other guys were watching over him. They weren't planning on stopping him either. Sincere and Stipes were staring down at him. I handed Stipes my weapon and approached Matthews slowly. "Petty Officer Matthews, stand down." I ordered. He continued stabbing and ignored me. Dragon and Judah came down with their guns drawn.

"What the fuck?" Judah whispered. I took a step forward and tried to reach Matthews again.

"Petty Officer Matthews, stand down." I said again with authority. He stopped and turned towards me slowly. Once his eyes were on me, it was like looking in a mirror. He was fighting a losing battle with keeping the sanity that he had when he enlisted. He was struggling with finding his purpose as a Seal, a human being, and a fucking monster. "Let's go, Matthews." I told him.

He stared up at me with a blank stare. I motioned for the other men to release the women and the children. Roc and Tags were hesitant, but left with the rest of the men. I squatted down and held my hand out for the knife. Matthews placed it in my hand and looked back at the dead man.

"I always wanted to know what the difference between them and us was. They took orders from men higher than them and killed the innocent. We do the same Davis. We do the exact same thing and call ourselves soldiers." He said and stood up.

"They are innocent, Matthews. The women and children in that room are who we here for." I replied. He looked at me and shook his head. We had been killing people for so long that sometimes I questioned the people that we killed. I felt myself losing the battle between what was my reality and the reality that the military wanted to cover up. It confused us all and made us kill like Matthews had. Sincere and Stipes pulled me off that ledge many of times and I had to do the same for them.

Matthews walked out the door still confused. Stipes began to walk out with the children and the women following behind them. I kicked the dead body over to hide the man's wounds. They didn't need to know that they were being rescued from monsters, by monsters. Tags and Rocs followed behind the women.

"Where did Matthews go?" Tags asked.

"What happened to Flex?" I asked instead.

"Sniper." Geronimo answered.

"Where," I turned towards him.

"We don't know." Tags answered. "I am going to go and check on Matthews." He said and walked out.

I looked at Geronimo and Rocs and knew that something was off about the whole situation. I wasn't going to say more about it until I talked to the rest of the team. I turned and walked out with Stipes and Sincere.

"I don't know about this, Davis. Dexter and I scoped this place out down to Domingo's men's bathroom breaks. Something else is going on here." Stipes said.

"I know. We'll all meet up at 2300 hours. Judah," I called out. Judah ran over to me with Dragon. "I want you with Matthews and the rest of the group."

"Aye, Aye." He answered and got in the van with them.

I walked over to Flex's body. He had a shot to the back of his head. The distance was far enough for it to be a sniper, but the shit could have been manipulated easily. I didn't want to think that, but the way they dismissed the Squad Leader's death rubbed me the wrong way. I squatted down and pulled his tags from around his neck. It was something that I knew that his son would have wanted.

"I can't believe this shit man. We have dealt with a lot of shit in our years together. Some missions, we knew that it was a probability of us not walking out alive. This shit was nothing, Man. We shouldn't have lost him like this." Sincere said.

He was right. The mission before that one, Sincere got shot in the chest and leg. The muthafucker was coughing up blood and everything. We barely made it back to get him the help that he needed. And that was in Afghanistan. How the fuck was I supposed to explain this shit to my

CO?

Dex pulled up on two wheels, pissed. I opened the door and he jumped in the back to work on his computer.

"They're wrong, Davis. I know that I didn't miss anything. I checked all perimeters before checking in with you and I didn't see shit." He said while punching on his keys. Sincere jumped in the driver's seat.

"Pull up the last camera feed right before they went in." I told him.

The ride back to headquarters wasn't that far. The building was surrounded by a metal gate and guards with guns. It was three buildings on the compound. One was for our sleeping quarters, the café, and other recreational shit that they do. The other was for medical and an interrogation rooms. The main building is where meetings were held and other offices.

When we pulled up, Judah jumped out and shook his head. He was letting me know that they didn't say anything about Flex.

"2300 hours." I yelled to them.

Matthews got out of the car and began to stare at the victims that were saved from the house, walking into the interrogation building. He took a step towards them.

"Hey, Matthews. Get cleaned up for the meeting." I yelled out. He turned and looked at me with those same dead eyes. He smirked at me and walked off. I went straight to my CO and told them everything that went down. They didn't believe the shit about Flex either. I told them that I was holding a meeting to get everybody's stories straight. They dismissed me and told me to meet back up with them in the morning.

I went to my area to get cleaned up, when Dexter came knocking on my door. I only had on a pair of pants and some socks. I opened the door and he walked in with his laptop. "I knew I didn't fuck up, J. Them muthafuckers planned this shit." He said.

"What are you talking about?" I asked him.

He sat his laptop on the small table in my room. He started pressing keys and turned it my way. Flex's back was turned towards the opening, but I only saw Tags, Rocs, and Geronimo. Matthews was nowhere in sight. I sat and watched as they talked it up with Flex, distracting him from what was coming to him. Two minutes in the video, we saw a flash and Flex went down. No one reacted to it. They stood and waited for the shooter to come out of hiding. Matthews came walking out with a sniper rifle. He began to give hand signals and orders. The guys nodded and moved in the house without word. "Where was this camera located?" I asked Dex.

"I always put out secret cameras so that I can get more than three angles. Tags was with me when I set up the cameras in the back. Those cameras were taken out right before the shooting start." He told me as he pulled up the different screens that were disconnected. Matthews' punk ass killed Flex. I didn't want to turn his ass in. I wanted to kill him myself. I looked up at Dexter and he already knew what I wanted to do.

"If we take him out, we will have to take them all out." He said.

An alarm started going off and guns were being fired. I grabbed my gun and ran out my room with Dexter behind me. Stipes and Sincere were running out their room towards the gunfire. "What's going on?" Dragon asked pulling up to the right of us.

"We don't know." Dexter said. I took lead and went to the front door of our building. They had a couple of guys standing by the door and one laying on the ground outside of it.

"Man, your team has gone crazy, Davis. Matthews is out there shooting people up and shit. Tags and Roc are flanking him. What the fuck is going on?" Petty Officer Martin asked. I looked out the door and saw that Geronimo was standing in the middle of the buildings with a gun pointed towards the building that we were in.

"We are going to hit the side doors. Petty Officer Martin and Petty Officer Porter, distract Geronimo." I told them and ran off to the side doors on the west side of the building. I peeked out and saw Roc with his gun up. I didn't know how many people they had on their crew now. But, Matthews left his main guys on us. He had to know that Roc and Geronimo couldn't fuck with the rest of the team. Don't get me wrong, them bitches had their shit in order. But, Stipes and Sincere alone could have taken out Matthew's team. I was about to push the door open and Roc took a step back. I closed the door and looked around the frame. There were wires hanging from the top of the door. Wires that weren't there before.

"This muthafucker set up a bomb at this door. I don't know how big it is, but if we open this door, it might take out the whole west side." I said. "We gotta get out of here." If this door was wired, I knew the rest of them were as well. I wasn't going to chance. "Stipes, run back to the front and alert the guys about the wiring. After that, come downstairs to the laundry room to go through the tunnel. I don't think they know anything about that." I said.

"What fucking tunnel?" Sincere's ass said. He wasn't good with tight and small spaces.

"Stop being a pussy." Dragon told him and led the way to the basement. Only a few of us knew about that spot. It was behind one of the dryers in the laundry room. The dryer that was always out of order. I pulled it from the wall with Sincere's help. Stipes came into the laundry room with more guns. He was always about his weapons. I didn't know who was worse out of him and Sincere. Dragon was our Asian buddy. He didn't like guns but was forced to carry one. He taught me how to use my blade.

"Stipes, I told you about them weapons in your room, Man." I scolded.

"They weren't in my room." He said and passed off one of his cold ass burners. The shit looked like it would promise a muthafucker a closed casket funeral.

"How do we know that Matthews doesn't know anything about this?" Sincere asked.

"Because I kept the monitors on this spot. No one went out or came in." Dexter said. I led them through the tunnel 'til we came to the end. There were only two ways that we could have went. Left, to the building that we host all the meetings. Right, was to the medic building and the other injured soldiers.

"Dragon and Stipes go left and check on the COs' and check to see if any of them are hurt. We are going to check on the survivors. Dex, you get to the main office and get into the computer cameras there.

Cut the lights off and seal the doors. The only way out will be through this tunnel. If you guys don't find anything, make sure you stay at the end of the tunnel. If you see any of them bitches, light their asses up." I told them. We went in different directions and continued until we hit another wall. It had a coding pad hooked up to it. I punched in the code and the door opened. It was in the basement of the building.

I opened the door and peeped out of it to see if there was anyone in the hall. Once I saw that there was no one visible, I walked out the room with Sincere watching my back. We heard more shots rang out. We took the stairs up to the third floor where the victims were. We needed to get them out of there before that nigga lost it completely.

We got to the third floor and heard voices. I nodded at Sincere and we both put our guns down. We don't want to make any noise and alert the others that was on the floor. The door opened and two Petty Officers walked out with their guns. I grabbed the gun from the solider and smashed it in his face. Then I grabbed his throat and snapped it. Sincere pulled the soldier's knife from his waist and stabbed him in his forehead. We placed their bodies on the ground and picked up our weapons. We walked out of the door and made a right to where more shots were going off. I walked past one of the interrogation rooms and heard Matthews talking.

I tapped on the door and waited for it to open. Tags opened it and Sincere blew his face off. I pushed through the door and saw Matthews standing over the children. The women that we brought there were dead. Matthews didn't look back. He kept talking to the children as if we didn't bust in that muthafucker. Judah was laying on the ground with his neck snapped. He must have tried to stop them before it started. That was going to be something else he paid for. I raised my gun up, pointing it at his head.

"Drop your fucking gun Matthews."

He finally looked over at me. There was no confusion there. His mind was made up to do what he came there to do. I didn't want to shot him. No. I wanted to kill him with my bare hands. They killed Flex like some fucking cowards. They didn't have the nuts to confront him like a man. Sincere's eyes were as dead as mine. He didn't know what happened, but he saw what his ass did.

"I had to do this. You have to know that this had to be done. They don't need to live with what happened to them. Bad dreams and growing up to be killers. Future soldiers would have to hunt these lil fuckers down and stop them from turning out other children. We have the power to stop this shit now. You know more than me what they will become. This is the right thing to do." He said to me. "Or they could end up like me. Like us." He continued. "We don't need another me or you out here, Jason."

I understood what he was saying. No matter what type of therapy those children go through, their mind was officially fucked up. I could see the fear in some of their eyes, but the others were staring at Matthews daring him to shoot. They were begging for death with their eyes. He saw it and wanted to give them that. But, it wasn't his place. If we had to deal with the consequences of our actions, oh well. That still didn't give that bitch the right to take their lives, Flex, and the other soldiers that died today because of what he thought was right.

I pulled out my hand gun and shot him in the hand that was holding his gun. He dropped it and tried to pick it up with his left hand. I tackled his ass to the ground and began to pound that fool in the face. Sincere was leading the children away from the brutal sight. I was hitting that nigga so hard that I heard some of my bones breaking. I didn't let that stop me though. His ass was going to feel his life slipping away, just like his victims did. I raised my hand to deliver the final blow and got tackled to the ground. I punched the guy in his face and tried to get back to a non-moving Matthews. I got pulled back by three other guys. Sincere ran over and knocked one of them out with one punch and began to beat on the other. I stood toe to toe with one of my COs.

"ET1, stand down. I repeat. Stand. Down." He said, but I wasn't hearing him.

"That muthafucker needs to be put down." I said angrily.

"He will get dealt with. You need to stand down and tell your soldier to stand down as well." He told me.

I looked back and Sincere had his weapon pointed at the CO. My dawg wasn't going to let nothing happen to me. He was ready to die in that room for me. But, I couldn't let him do that. I knew that his baby sister would kill me if something happened to him. She was all he had. I placed my hand on the gun and pushed it down.

"Stand down, Sin." I told him. He dropped his weapon, but was ready to square up.

"Get that piece of shit out of here." My CO told the MPs that were waiting for orders. They picked Matthews up and carried him out of the room. Sincere walked up and stood by my side. Dexter, Dragon, and Stipes was standing by the door. "Meet me in the next room." The CO said to us and walked past the rest of my team. They all looked at me and waited for me to give them the "ok". I nodded my head and we followed him into the other room. They had four other officers present. They were all standing at the other end of the table like they knew what was going on next door and didn't give a fuck.

"You and the rest of your team will go to Texas where Nicholas Domingo is hiding at. You will bring him back here alive." The CO spoke.

"You knew that he wasn't here the whole time. Why are we here?" I asked without all of the other pleasantries.

"That is not your concern ET1 Davis. You have your orders. You and your team need to be in the air in fifteen." He said and then dismissed us. I knew that, that was going to be my last mission. They were planning shit and didn't let us know what the fuck was going on. I wasn't going to let my brothers die over some shit that I didn't even understand. What fuck me up more was when I hesitated to kill Matthews. I considered what he was saying and that wasn't something that I could tell anyone. I knew that I was falling into a place where I wouldn't be able to come back from. After we secured Nicholas Domingo, the rest of my team resigned and we went our separate ways.

1
JASON

I pulled over when I heard the name of Sierra's brother. The last I heard of Matthews was that they put his ass on another mission with a new team. He took them all out and went into hiding. Now, the muthafucker was in my city, looking for revenge on his stupid ass family. I redialed Dex's number and it went to voicemail. He told me not to come because they had his house surrounded. I needed to know who "they" was. I pulled off and made an illegal U-turn. I dialed Tristan's number and waited for him to answer.

"Man, what the fuck do you want at this time of hour, Jason." He said groggily.

"Get your ass up. I need you to pull up the last feed from Dex's cameras. Matthews got in his house, without setting off any alarms. After he left, he blew the house up." I told him.

"WHAT? The fuck are you talking about. Are you saying Dex is dead, Bruh?" Tristan screamed.

"I don't know." I responded.

"But you said his house blew up. You said-", I interrupted him.

"I know what the fuck I said Tristan. Just do what I asked you. I am on my way to you now." I told him and hung up to dial Joel's number. I needed to get Tyja on this as well.

"What's wrong?" Joel answered.

"I need you to call Tyja and tell her to meet us over at Tristan house. I will explain what is happening when you get there. Also, get your brothers over there. It's serious. El." I told her.

"Alright Jason. We are on the way." She said and hung up. We were staying in the house that her brothers and father lived in. We were getting her dream house built on the north side of Philly. We were going to build a small estate where we was all going to have a house. Joel wanted us to be close, so that the kids could grow up with each other. Ma thought it was a good idea as well. Her house was going to sit at the end of the estate. Kymani and Kymel's house was going to be the first ones you pass going into the estate. If anyone wanted trouble they had to be some bad niggas to get past them crazy muthafuckers. Callum also was going to have a house there. He wasn't going to be there often, because of his businesses in Jamaica. I dialed one more number before reaching Tristan.

"Yo," Jo answered.

"Meet me by Tristan." I told him and hung up without listening to his response. I pulled up to Tristan's home in the suburbs. His home was set up like Dex's. There was some type of electronic set up in each room. Tristan took it to a whole new level though. He had an invisible laser. Once we stepped onto the sidewalk in front his house, all the cameras would beep and zoomed in on that person. He was going to build that on all of our properties. I stepped out of my car and headed to the front door. The door opened by itself. It usually did that when I or any of the other family members came through. I walked in and went straight to the basement where I knew his ass was going to be.

"Were you able to pull up anything?" I asked.

"Yeah, Man. I was able to pull up a lot of shit. I saw the house exploding too, without Dexter making it out." He said with anger.

"Dex is alive Tristan. Don't worry about that right now. I just need you to focus on the niggas that was with Matthews." I said and took a seat next to him. I watched the feed from the cameras and saw three guys with him. I wasn't surprised seeing Roc and Geronimo with him. There were three other people with him that I didn't know.

"See if you can find out who those three are?" I asked while looking at the other footage. I saw the men cut the wires to the camera and setting up the bomb that went off. "Pull the cameras from the inside." I told him.

He pulled that up and we saw Matthews trying to get into Dex's system. You had to be the shit to break that nigga's system. We saw him trying and failed. He pulled out his phone and began to talk to someone. He pulled out a flash drive and plugged it in the computer. He began to type and looked like he was getting everything he needed out of the computer.

"How is it that he is able to get this shit off the computer without unlocking it?" I asked Tristan.

"The shit is easy. If someone is having technical difficulty with their computers, they will call for help. They ask you shit like, what type of computer it is or what Wi-Fi they are under. But, Dexter didn't keep shit like that on the computer that he is on now. He had all that type of information on jump drives, which are locked up in the house. After every mission, he would erase it from his hard drive. Whatever they are downloading, is not going to help them." The computer started beeping and I saw my girl walking towards the door, with both of our brothers and Tyja in tow. Tank's ass was pulling up in the driveway. Tristan pressed a button to let them in. Tank got out of his car and led the gang downstairs. Joel walked over to me with her hair up in a ponytail. She had on a wife beater and some tights. I had to ignore what she was doing to me and focus on what was going on.

"What happened?" She asked.

I took a deep breath before responding. "Dexter called me and told me that Matthews was in his house. Matthews was the soldier that I almost tried to kill because of some fucked up shit he did. We thought the military was going to put him away, instead they used his anger and technique and put him on more missions. The last mission he was on, he killed everyone on his team and went AWOL."

"Ok, so why is he here now. To get revenge on you." JJ asked.

"Yes, but not because of what happened years back. He is angry about losing his family."

"And they were?" Jo asked.

I looked at Joel before saying. "Sierra and her brothers."

"Damn!" Jo said. The computers started beeping again and we all were on guard. Everyone that I asked to be here, was here.

"That is not for this property." Tristan said. Tyja was already on her laptop, trying to figure out who the other three were that was with Matthews. Tristan pulled up the cameras that was by the Center. He zoomed in and saw some of our men dead on the ground.

"Fuck, Bruh! That's Wilson, Marquel's cousin." Jo said. Marquel and Malik was going to lose it. Wilson was the only family that they dealt with on their father's side. He introduced Wilson to Jordan some years back. Wilson wanted to work with them in the guns business, but Don wasn't having it. We saw some men coming out of the Center. I saw Matthews walking towards the camera. He looked up in it and smirked.

"Davis. I know you are watching this and trying to figure out why I am doing this. And it's simple. My sister Sierra is one reason. My brothers were ok but my sister was my heart and you took her from me. When I heard that she was dating you, I knew that she was going to end up dead. I couldn't save her. Just like you couldn't save Flex, Judah, or Dexter. You also won't be able to save Jordan, Joseph, or Ms. Joyce. Everything with the Davis name on it, I will destroy.

I heard that your family has a lot of businesses around the area, so I thought that it would be right if I started off with the place you killed my brothers and father. Speaking of fathers, I heard that you are one. Congratulations. I hope you spend as much time with them as possible. I told you before that the world didn't need another you or me in it. So, I will be coming for them as well. I also heard that the Elites were friends of yours. I have something for them as well.

Sierra ordered a hit for them to take you out, and she gets killed right after that. You can let them know that the Eliria's Gang is coming for them. It's a favor that they owe me. Now that all of my cards are on the table, let's get this shit started. Roc." He said. Roc held up his phone and pressed the star button. The Center blew up with the dead bodies around it. Matthews and his men began to laugh and jumped in their trucks. Tristan zoomed in on their license plates. Tyja began to punch in some keys and it came up stolen.

"I found out who the other three are. Jonathan Edwards is the tall black man. He is from Queens, New York. He joined the Army six years ago and was discharged for knocking out his lieutenant. He has an older brother that teaches at NYU. He has no kids and both parents are dead. The other man is Luis Domingo. He is the son of Nicholas Domingo. After your team snatched his father up, he left college to resume his father's activities. He has an empire in Mexico with his new wife and children. The last man is..." She paused and waited for the picture to upload. When it did, Kymani and Kymel stepped forward.

"Muthafucker." Kymani said.

"You know this dude." I asked him.

"Yeah. That is Badrik Dixion. He is one of my father's ex-mistress' kid. She tried to pin her son on Pops, but he told her that he wasn't his. He took the paternity test and it came out negative. Three years ago, he came to Pops for a job. He wanted to be trained as one of the Elites. Pops told him no and offered him another job. He didn't want it and caused a scene at Pops' business. Pops removed him and we hadn't seen him since. They know that Pops work with the Elites. They don't know that we are the Elites. I gotta call Pops." Kymani finished and walked off.

El was quiet and that wasn't a good thing. Her demeanor changed when he threatened our children. She was thinking of ways to get to him before any of us and that shit wasn't going to fly. The shit was going to be dealt with by all of us. I didn't want my family involved. If I lose them on some shit, I wasn't going to be able to come back from it. It was time for me to reach out to my Seal brothers. They were trained to deal with Roc and Geronimo.

"Who are the Eliria's gang?" Jo asked.

El took in a deep breath and closed her eyes. She was trying to calm herself before talking. "Eliria's gang are a group of assassins in France." She said and opened her eyes. She walked over to Tyja and tapped her on the shoulder. Tyja began typing on her keyboard and pulled up the gang on the TV screen. It was a woman and two men. The woman was white with a slender face, green eyes, and red hair. She was sitting and wearing a black fitted dress, with red shoes. The two men that were standing behind her looked like twins. They both had red hair and green eyes. They looked like they stood over six feet with broad shoulders. They were in black suits with red ties. The only way that you can tell the difference between the two was that one of them had a large tattoo on his neck of a Thor's Hammer.

"Eliria's Gang is her and her two brothers. Eliria, whose assassin name is Storm, started out when her mother tried to have her father killed. She didn't want her children to grow up like him, so she ordered our Poppa to do it. Before Poppa could agree to the shit, Eliria cut off her mother's head and sent it to my father. She told him that they will take care of their own business. Eliria was fifteen at the time. Once they father found out, he sent his children to some of the best trainers that their money could buy.

Antoine and Enzo, her brothers, were hired to take out a rat. He was supposed to testify against one of the largest crime families in France. The brothers decapitated his head and the heads of the men in his family. They then placed the heads on the picket fence of the DA's yard. After that, a criminal named Luciano Dubois put in an order to kill off the whole police unit. He wanted it brutal and bloody. No one wanted to take the job at first and Luciano didn't want to hire newbies. He wanted professionals that wouldn't get caught. Eliria's dad, Rapheal Cassel, told him that his children would get the job done. Luciano believed him because of the clout that the Cassel name carried and the previous job they finished. They didn't disappoint. They painted the station with the blood of those officers. The ones that were off was killed with their families. That was what put their names into the assassin world." Joel said.

"They have businesses like trading companies, clothing lines, and other fancy bullshit. Everyone in France know who they were and follow by their rules." Kymel finished with his head down. He was also trying to calm himself down.

"I know that they heard about y'all. Why agree to this shit?" Tank asked.

"Because they want to be the best and in order to do that, you have to defeat the champs." Kymani walked in and answered. "They been asking for it. If this is how they want to do, so be it." He continued and looked at Joel and Kymel. "Pops wants us back to Jamaica, now." Kymani and Kymel dapped us off and walked out of the door.

Joel walked up to me shaking her head. "I will take the kids and the women with me. Once we find out more, I'll be back. Don't move without me, Jason." She said.

"I can't sit still Joel and let this muthafucker destroy everything we worked for. Everything that my father built." I told her. I knew what she was saying, but I wasn't going to sit here and wait for that muthafucker to come to me. If anything, I was going to take the fight to him.

"I am not asking you to hide or sit and wait, Jason. When you come up with a plan, let me know and I am on my way. I have to get our children to safety first. I know that you have back-up in mind, but none of them muthafuckers is going to have your back like me. Alright." Joel said with her angry eyes. She was right though. My girl didn't trust no one. I placed my hand on her face and brought her closer. I kissed her lips softly.

"Hurry back, El." I told her. She wrapped her arms around mine and pulled me in for another kiss. After she got her fill, she pulled back and gazed up into my eyes. "Be safe." She said and stepped back. She looked around the room and smiled. "All of you be safe. Don't go anywhere by yourselves and keep the watch on at all times. If y'all see anything suspicious, don't try to be a fucking hero. Call the shit in and wait for help. Tyja, don't leave the house without two guards. I will send more men down here for your disposal." Joel said. She turned back to me and kissed me again. She nodded her head and walked out the door.

"What is the first move?" Jo asked. I walked and stood behind Tristan.

"We gotta close all of our businesses down. Let the employees know that we are having technical difficulties and that they will be on leave with pay. Give all the waitress and waiters that work at the restaurants and bars a bonus check and tell them that business won't resume until further notice. We don't want none of our employees dying for some shit that they don't have nothing to do with." I told them.

"We have to find out where those assholes are staying. I want receipts from the last three weeks and flight information. I want to know where they came from before they got here and if they have people working in the background. The Elites will give us more information about Eliria's Gang. Make the calls that need to be made and go pack some clothes. I will text y'all the destination." I told them. I walked out the front door looking around to see if those niggas were here. I knew that Matthews was going to lay low for a couple of days before striking again. We had to be ready for whatever that fool was bringing. I jumped in my car and started making my phone calls. The phone began to ring, as I headed towards my destination.

"What's up J? You back in my city?" Sincere asked. We haven't talked since my father's funeral. Stipes was also there for support and ready to bust some heads with me. I told them that I was cool and that everything was already done.

"Naw, but I need you here in mine. Matthews is here with Geronimo and Roc. The chick that put a hit out on my fam was his sister." I told him. I took in a deep breath before releasing the other news. I knew that he wasn't gone, but if Sincere was to come here and not see Dex, he was going to flip out. "He got to Dex and blew his house up, with him in it." I finished.

I heard horns blowing and knew that, that nigga was sitting in the middle of the street. "Did you find the body?" He asked.

"No, but he told me that he was going to send me his location." I replied. I heard someone talking in the background.

"Hey muthafucker. You want to move your silly ass out the fucking street. Pull over and do that shit, Bruh." I heard.

"Hold on, J," Sin replied with no emotions. "Get. The. Fuck. Away. From. My. Shit." He told the guy. I didn't need to be there to know that he didn't have a gun. The nigga could spear you with a look and have you shaking for dear life.

"My bad, Dawg. You got that." The man told him.

"I'll call Stipes and inform him of everything. We all should be there tomorrow night. Text me where." He said and hung up. I knew that Stipes was going to be down for the mission. Dragon took an oath to not kill again. I respected his mind and kept my distance from him. I didn't want to provoke his killer instinct. I went through my phone and pulled up Marquel's number. I had to let him know that his cousin died and ask him to meet me at my place. No one knew where we got our weapons from. They thought that my connection was someone connected to military.

"What's up wit cha?" Marquel answered.

"Are you in my city?" I asked.

"No, but I can be. What you need?" He replied.

"The chief's special." I told him. That was our code words for war time. I didn't need that little shit unless it was hitting those fools hard. "We got hit today, Quel. They hit the Center where Wilson was working and he didn't make it."

"Hold up. Hold up. What did you say?" Marquel got serious. He was always about his business but when he came to his family, that nigga would lose it.

"Your cousin Wilson died this morning." I told him.

"I am on my way." He said. I hung up the phone and threw it in the passenger's seat. After all this shit was over, I was going on a vacation. Fuck that. There was no way that my family had that much bad luck. Matthews was as crazy as I was if he thought that he was going to come to my city, bossing up. He hadn't seen the unleashed Jason. He only saw the muthafucker that I wanted them to see. There was nothing that was going to prepare him for what he was about to get into.

I pulled up at a large apartment building around Parkside. It was a surrounded by security gate. I pulled out my card and swiped it through the security pad. The light flashed green and the gate opened up with three guards standing in front of my car. I rolled my window down and drove in. Charlie stepped to the window.

"There will be some company coming through here. If the name is not on my family list, don't let them through. I need everyone, including Mr. Lampos, to the main room in twenty minutes." I told them and pulled off.

The apartment building was four floors with a workout room, indoor and outdoor pool, a small park area for the kids and daycare center. I also had a cleaning service that cleaned the apartments three times a week. These apartments were set up for single parents that were hard on their luck. Rent was based on how much they were able to afford. I pulled up to the main office and reached for my phone. I sent the address to my family in a text. Before I got to the door, the security team was walking up. It was sixteen of them. Once Sincere and Stipes got here, they were going to take the lead with them, so that I can focus on Matthews.

I opened the door and waited 'til everybody was in before I started talking. My office was a wide opened space. It had a big ass wooden L-shape desk on the back wall. There was a sofa set and a few more chairs in the room. There were two smaller desks in the corner for the owners. We had televisions on the wall and a small bar area for myself. I knew that I was going to need a drink dealing with the tenants in that place.

"We have a situation. With that being said, Charlie, I need you to put the guards on code red until my boy arrives. Everyone stay in contact and at your post. If any of you leave your post at any time, I will kill you. Is that understood?"

"Yes, Sir." They all answered. Mr. Lampos walked in with the head of my cleaning services, Ms. Janet.

"Mr. Davis," They greeted.

"My family is coming here. Make sure that the rooms on the fourth floor are in good shape. They are not coming with a lot of shit, so they need towels, toilet paper, and all that other shit to make them comfortable. Mr. Lampos, you can use the business card to go and grab these things. They will be here in an hour." I told them. They nodded and walked out the door with the security team. I sat behind my desk and pulled up all the cameras that was surrounding the property. Everything was looking good so far.

I turned in my seat and pressed in my code. The left side of the room wall went up. There were guns, knives, grenades, and cash. I pulled out my two twenty-two's and placed them both in my gun holsters. I grabbed some cash and shut the wall back down. We wouldn't be able to use our cards anymore. I didn't want to make it easy for that bitch to find us. I walked over to my phone and picked it up.

It was Mason facetiming me. I knew that he was going to call. He became a Daddy's boy quick. Everywhere I went, he was there right by my side, asking questions and taking notes. He was going to be one of those silent killers, like his mom. He sat back and observed shit before acting. Madison, on the other hand, always tried to find different angles to help the person change or live. If she could make them see things her way, she would let them live, but would make it difficult for them to enjoy life. She'll cut off a limb or make the person blind.

I answered the phone and saw my lil man. "What's up Lil Man?"

"Dad, why I couldn't stay with you?" He asked.

"Because I need you to protect your sister and your Grandma. You already know this, so why ask." I asked him.

He sighed and put his head down. "Dad, she has Mom and my uncles here. She was going to be fine. You don't have nobody there watching your back." He said.

"JJ, Jo, and Tank is here Mason. I also called up some of my military brothers to pass through. I'm good son." I told him. I saw that he was holding something back still. I sat down and pulled the phone up to my face. "What's really wrong with you son?" I asked him.

He looked up with sadness in his eyes. I haven't seen that before, so I was nervous to hear his response. "I don't know. I mean. I just got you back. I don't want to lose you, Dad. You are my best friend, besides JoJo and Madison. I don't think that I would be able to be strong enough if something happens to you." He told me.

That shit hit home, for real. We never had talks about shit like this or if something ever happened to me. I didn't want to have this conversation with him over the phone. The only thing that I was able to do at that moment was to ease his mind until I saw him again. "I'll tell you what Lil Man. When Mommy come back, I'll make sure that she brings you and Madison with her so that we can talk ok." I told him.

His face lit up quick with that answer. "Aight, bet. Love you Dad." He said.

"Love you, too. Where is your mother?" I asked him.

"She is in the front with Uncle Mel and Mani. Do you want me to put her on?" He replied.

"Yeah, put her on right quick." I told him. He got up from his seat and showed me a sleeping Madison. My baby girl looked like an Angel. Her hair was all over her head and she was holding onto her doll that I bought her.

"Ma, Dad want to speak to you." Mason said and passed Joel the phone. Her pretty face filled the screen. She always had ways of pulling smiles out of me at any time of the day, no matter what we were going through.

"Hey, Baby." I spoke.

"Hey. You look tired. You need to get some rest because the next few days are going to be rough." She said.

"You know that I won't be able to sleep without you by my side. Did you find out anything else about Badrik?" I asked her.

"Nothing yet. Pops is planning on going over there to see his mother with my Godfather. He is hoping to find out what made him do this. Either way, Badrik will still die." She said with no expression on her face, but her eyes was telling me everything. She already knew how she was going to kill him. "Where are you?" She asked. I knew that she was looking at the big ass picture of Mason and Madison on the wall behind me.

"I am at the apartment building." I told her.

"That's great. It has enough rooms for everyone and he wouldn't find it. I have a few guards headed your way. Let your team know so that they can let them in." She said.

"I will. You know I meant what I said." I told her. She looked like she didn't understand what I was talking about. "Hurry up back." I continued.

She smiled that sweet smile and nodded her head. "You got that, Baby. I love you." She told me.

"I love you, too. See you soon." I told her and hung up. My office door opened with a knock. "You good." Tank walked in.

"Yeah, I'm straight. Come on in." I stood and walked around the table. Tank walked in carrying a duffle bag and some other shit that was probably for Tristan. Tank placed the laptop bag carriers on the floor and took a seat on the couch that was in my office.

"Man, this shit is nice. I didn't know you had this." Tank told me, while looking around my office. Tristan came in with his bags. I went to hold the door open for my brothers and Tyja. JJ dropped his bags and went straight to the bar. Jo and Tristan was looking at the television that was mounted on the wall.

"Hey, J. When did you get this?" JJ asked, while fixing him another drink.

"I started building this when I found out about the twins." I answered.

"You know that fool is coming for this, too." Jo answered.

"No he won't. This is not in my name. This is under M&M Company." I answered, walking back to my desk.

"Who the fuck runs the M&M Company? I never heard of them?" Tristan said frowning.

"M&M stands for Mason and Madison. Jason put the building under their name so that they can have something of their own when they get older. He also have stocks and bonds under their company names as well. When the twins get older, they wouldn't want for nothing. They are already multimillionaires." Tyja said while walking over to JJ.

"Man, that's tight, Bruh." Jo answered. They set up a trust fund for JoJo and Jerimiah. That shit could easily run out. I wanted my children to have money flowing from all directions. And if my plan A, B, C, D, and E fell off. Joel had other shit under their name and ready to pick up where I left off.

"It was Joel's idea." I told everybody.

"That's smart, Man. Do y'all have an accountant?" Jo asked.

"Yeah. Kymani." I told him. They all looked surprised. Kymani and Kymel were Accountants and had a CPA firm based in New York. They were some smart ass niggas. They schooled Joel and she was passing the information on to our children.

"I will have to talk to them when they get back. And you know after we finish this shit." He said. Ms. Janet walked in with the keys to the apartments that my family would be staying in. She gave them their individual keys and asked them to follow her to their rooms. I got up and went behind them to get settled in my own room. That was the only thing that we were able to do at the moment. I watched my brothers' faces as a portrait of our parents were seen in the lobby. Pops was holding Ma and smiling down at her, as she looked into the camera. There was so much love that we saw in that picture.

"You know that he would have been proud of us right now. He would have spoiled our kids?" Jo said smiling.

"No doubt. He would have loved Maddie, man." I told him. My dad always wished that he had a daughter. When Ma pushed out them three boys, he was like fuck it, don't worry about it. JJ shook his head.

"Yeah, Kymel and Kymani little sparring sessions would have been different. He would have been shot their asses." He said laughing.

"You ain't never lying." Jo said and picked his bag up. I walked them to the elevator and we went up to the fourth floor to get some rest.

2

JOEL

We arrived at my father's house five hours after leaving Philly. My mind was racing. I didn't know nothing about this other woman or her son, Badrik. I didn't know why Pops cared enough to go and talk to the woman. Kymani was carrying Madison in, while Mason and Kymel grabbed the bags. Ma-Ma was carrying little Jerimiah. My brothers stopped and looked up to the sky. Mason stopped and looked back at the gate.

Ma-Ma stopped with Lily and glanced down at Mason. "What's wrong Mace?" She asked him. Mason turned around and smiled at his Grandmother. "Nothing grandma cum wi guh inna di yaad." He told her. Ma-Ma turned around and began walking in the house. She told us how Mason acted before they were kidnapped. She understood that he was feeling something and that it was time for them to get their ass in the house.

I felt the uneasiness in the air, but knew that we had time to prepare for whatever. I walked in and stopped when I noticed that T Glen was standing outside. She pulled out her cigarettes and stood by the fountain. I walked over to her and sat next to her.

"You good Teedy?" I asked. She placed the cigarette in her mouth and pulled on it. She blew the smoke in the air like she was releasing her last breath.

"We are getting too old for this shit. I always thought that after I passed the business on to my sons, I was going to be able to live freely. I feel like I am in deeper than I was before. I want to retire from this shit all the way. I don't want to have to worry about muthafuckers coming after me over some dumb shit, ya know." She said to me. I nodded my head, understanding everything that she was saying. It was hard to leave the business without repercussions or people testing you to see if you are still dangerous. The shit was getting old and tiring. We all had so much to live for and this business wasn't in my future. I was planning on protected my family at all cost and leaving the other shit behind.

"I know Teedy. Hopefully after this is over, we can all go on a vacation and chill. Hell, if you want, you, Ma-Ma and Lily can get on the plane right now. You guys can go wherever y'all want." I told her. She smiled at me.

"I can't leave my boys, Joel. Not my babies." She said and threw her cigarette on the ground. I stood and grabbed her hands.

"Mi nah let nothing happen to yuh boys. Mi put day pon mi life." I told her. Tank and Tristan were my family too. Once we got the information we needed, I was going to move full throttle with my plan.

She was worried. True.

But she had to understand that, they were going to work better if they knew that she was safe. She squeezed my hand and nodded her head.

"I'll think about it." She said and walked into the house. I motioned for the guards to close the gate, when I saw three SUVs pulling up on the outside of it. I walked back in the house like I didn't see them. I went to my father's office where my brothers were. My father was in his uniform, suit and tie. That was what my brothers and I called it. He was always sporting some type of suit from different designers.

"It looks like we have company." I told them. My Dad went to his security camera and saw that they were sitting by the gate, trying to figure out how they were going to get in. My father reached over and pressed a button on the intercom.

"Winston gwaan a break an tek di boys wid yuh." He told him.

"Boss dem get three trucks out here yuh kno." Winston replied.

"Yeah mi kno. Mi an di fambly wa fi let out sum stress. It been a rough week." He said. We watched as the men that were guarding our home jumped in their vehicles and pulled off. I didn't understand why he had guards here anyway.

My father looked back at us and smiled with a dead look. We knew what that meant. It was time to make some examples. Because clearly, they didn't know who they were fucking with. My brothers and I walked off calmly. There was no need to rush. I walked upstairs to check on my family. T Glen grabbed her gun and was ready.

"T Glen, I need you to stay up here with everyone else." I told her. She was about to say something but Ma-Ma stepped in.

"Go take care of your business, Baby. We will be ok." She said looking over at T Glen. I nodded and turned to see Madison and Mason standing at the door with their weapons. I saw in their eyes that it wasn't going to be easy to convince them that they couldn't come.

They both had their all black on with their Jordan nines. Madison was leaning against the wall flipping her knife. "Who wi a guh wid?" She asked.

"Madison, yuh guh wid Reap and Mason yuh guh wid Shadow. Listen to wah dem tell yuh." I said, pointing directly to Mason. Jason has been teaching Mason some new shit and I knew that he couldn't wait to try it on somebody. They nodded their head and went to find their uncles. I went to my room and changed my shoes from sandals to boots. I didn't have time to go into a wardrobe change like the twins. I grabbed my ponytail holder and a couple of my knives. I didn't like using guns unless it was totally necessary.

I walked back downstairs to rejoin my family. Daddy was leaning against the wall by the stairs, waiting for the exact moment to move. We all were patient like that. We didn't rush our kills. We enjoyed them. We liked watching assholes that wronged us in any way, suffer from small puncture wounds that was going to bleed out if they didn't get to a hospital within minutes. It was the thrill.

"Wah di fuck taking dem suh lang to find di lights? Di breaka right by di fucking gate." Kymani said. Kymel walked to the window with the lights on, not caring if they saw him. He shook his head and started laughing.

"Dem drive back to di gate. Mi guess dem neva seet pon dem way inna." Kymani replied. That meant that those fools didn't know what they were doing and didn't know who Callum was. Everyone on this fucking island knew who my father was.

"Fucking amateurs." Poppa spat out. He was insulted. He got up from the wall and stormed into his office. He was saying how he had to show muthafuckers who he was all over again. We heard shit being thrown and moved around in his office. We all were staring at the door. My father walked out with his shirt off and his dreads down. Poppa tattoos were looking fresh on his chest and arms. He had the first machete that was given to him, in his hand.

"Dem yah muthafuckas a guh learn todeh." He said angrily and walked to the backdoor. He swung it open and walked out cursing and growling. We stood and waited for Poppa to return. When we heard a gunshot, we walked out the front door and saw a guy standing in front of Poppa with his arm chopped off by the elbow. He was screaming and slinging blood everywhere. Another man ran behind Poppa and wrapped his arms around my Poppa's shoulders. Poppa threw his head back and hit the man in his face. He rose the machete up and slammed it into the foot of his assailant. The man dropped his arms from his shoulders. Poppa turned and pulled two knives from his back. He slammed the knives into the man ears and kicked the man in his chest, like he was the dude from *300*.

Two more men ran up on him and got closed line by his thick ass arms. When they tried to get up, Poppa began to kick their heads in the ground. We sat back and watched him release the built up anger that he had been holding in since we found out about his ex-girl. Mason and Madison started walking down the stairs. I was about to tell them something, 'til I realized where they were headed. The last of man in the group, tried to run when he saw that he wasn't a match for Poppa. He got to the SUV and started it up. The man backed up wildly and ran into the wall. Madison continued walking, while Mason stopped and held up his gun. He let off two shots, hitting the front tires. The back tires were stuck in the gutter. He pressed on the gas, but didn't move. The man jumped out of the car and tried to run to the gate. Madison threw a knife at the back of the man's knee.

"AHHHH," he yelled and fell down. He tried to crawl the rest of the way, but was stopped at the sight of Madison standing over him.

"Eff yuh chat to mi, mi promise dat mi nah let di men hurt yuh." She told him. He looked like he didn't understand what she was saying. She tried again in English and he still looked confused. Madison motioned her hand for the man to say something, so that she could see what language he spoke.

"Je ne comprends pas ce que vous dites. "(I don't understand what you are saying.) He said. I was all too familiar with that language. And if it was French that they were speaking, I knew that it was Eliria that sent those men to my father's house.

Madison stepped forward and pulled the knife out of the man's leg. He screamed and tried to back up from her. She held her hand up and shushed him. "Je ne vais pas faire du mal à vous, ami (e). Je l'ai dit, si vous nous Parlez, je vous promets que les hommes ne vous blessera pas. Mais, vous devez répondre à chaque question que nous demandons."(I am not going to hurt you, friend. I said if you talk to us, I promise you that the men won't hurt you. But, you have to answer every question we ask you.) Madison told him in a sweet tone. She talked to him and he listened.

His stupid ass nodded his head without hesitation. He was so busy trying to get away, that he didn't notice that it was the kids that stopped him from escaping. He also thought that it was the men that he needed to worry about it. Oh, how he was far from knowing the truth.

Mason walked and stood over the man with his sister. The man looked at him and turned his head back to my daughter. Mason shook his head and walked off.

"Him a coward Uncle. Di man couldn't look mi inna di yeye fi one minute. Mi a guh to bed." Mason said as he passed us to go into the house. He sounded disappointed. He was ready for the man to tell Madison no. Kymani and Kymel walked over to the man to pull him inside to talk. Poppa finished kicking the other men to death. He dropped his head back and inhaled the morning air. The sun was about to rise in a couple of seconds and we wanted to get to Badrik's mother's house before noon today. That meant, we needed to squeeze everything out of the little shit that my brothers was bringing in. Madison walked up to me and smiled.

"Is it ok if I sit in the interrogation?" She asked.

"Of course, Luvie." I said to her. She followed my brothers into the house as I stood and waited for my father. He stepped over the men and walked towards me, looking like my brothers. His dreads were dripping with blood and his body with sweat. I haven't seen my Poppa in action, in a long time. It was good to see that he still had it in him.

Once he was close, he glanced at me and smirked. "Wah yuh looking at child?" He said, devoid of emotions. My father brought me on a job with him to see if killing people was something that I wanted to do. He taught me how to be observant and to always expect the unexpected. He killed four men with a spiked iron whipped. Once he hit you with the whip, it rips off the skin that it is attached to. The men were on the ground bleeding out and dying slowly. I looked up at my Poppa at five years old, while he stared down on me. "Wah yuh looking at child?" He said in the exact same way, as he did when I was a little girl. I looked up at him and said the same thing I tell him every time he ask.

"Mi hero." I told him. He smiled at me and walked back in the house. He walked into his office and sat at his desk in front of the man that tried to get away. The man was shivering and looking over at Madison. He was hanging onto a promise that a little girl made him. She went and got some bandages and began to wrap the man's leg up. She asked Kymani to fix the man a drink. Kymani did so and handed it to him. Madison looked up and gave him a reassuring smile. She asked the man his name and he told her. "

Mon nom est Adam." He answered her.

"Hi, Adam. My name is Madison. That is my mother Joel, my two uncles Kymel and Kymani." She turned and head nodded in Poppa's direction. "That is my grandfather, Callum." She finished. Adam looked over at my father.

"Who send yuh?" My father asked, laying his machete on the desk. Kymani and Kymel stood back to let father take lead. The man still didn't know that he was standing in the room with the Elites. I stood on the side of the desk and leaned against the wall. Madison stepped forward and translated. We all knew how to speak French. We wanted him to maintain that bond with Madison. He responded and told her everything. You saw the changes in her eyes with every word he spoke. He wasn't paying attention. He kept running his mouth, digging his self in a bigger hole. Once he was finished, he looked around and waited for Madison to translate for us. When she didn't, he looked back at her and saw the dead eyes that didn't match the innocent girl before. He sat back in his seat and tried to find another exit strategy.

I stepped forward and sat on the end of the desk. "So, let me get this straight." I spoke in French. He looked at me with wide eyes. "Eliria sent your asses here to get information from my father, about the Elites. Once you got that information, you was to bring me to them to lure the Davis crew in. Does that sum it up?" I asked him. He looked over at my father and waited for him to react. But he didn't. He also didn't see the machete laying across the desk anymore. He looked back at Kymel and Kymani. They flashed that evil grin at him and took a step by the door. He took in a deep breath before answering.

"Oui. Eliria voulait Callum pour envoyer les élites pour vous sauver. J'ai aussi entendu que Badrik vous voulait pour lui-même. Il pensait que si vous en épousez lui, Callum n'aurait aucun autre choix, que de lui laisser l'entreprise." He whispered, knowing that he was going to get out here alive. That let me know that the guy was young and haven't done anything like this before.

I felt sorry for him. Not enough to let him live though. "Badrik wants to marry my sister so that he can ease his way into my father's business to take over it." Kymani asked. Adam nodded his head. Before Adam can say anything else, Madison raised the machete and chopped his head off. Adam's head flew over to Kymel. Madison was finished with that conversation a long time ago. The twins didn't play behind their parents and I'm pretty sure Mason would have been killed him. Madison placed Poppa's machete back on the table. We all looked over at Poppa to see what his reaction was going to be. We wasn't supposed to use other people weapons to make kills. Poppa was strict with us, about touching his weapons. Whatever it was that we wanted, he made sure we got it.

He smiled over at Madison and shook his head. "Yuh couldn't tek it no more huh Madison." He asked her. She looked at him and shook her head. She turned towards me with soft but angry eyes.

"Mi tink wi need fi tell daddy wah happen here." She said.

"I will tell him later. Right now I need you to go to upstairs and get cleaned up. You need to get some rest." I told her. She walked over to me and gave me hug. I bent down and kissed her on the forehead. She waved at everyone else and walked out the office. Poppa turned around in his chair and pressed the intercom button.

"Get rid of dem deh bodies pon mi lawn an di otha three inna di back. Send a team inna here to remove dis piece of shit outta mi office." He told his crew and stood. "Wait fi mi inna di fambly room mi need fi clean myself up Tell yuh Parrain fi get fi him ass of here now." Poppa told us and walked into his adjoining bathroom. We walked out his office and into the family room. The family room was the only room that didn't have windows. There was a sectional, bar and two love seats in the room. That room held so many memories. Good and bad. The room was filled with pictures of us when we were younger and up to the present. Madison and Mason pictures were on the wall by itself. Poppa always told us that we had to cherish them at that age. I sat in one of the love seats and pulled out my phone. I dialed my Parrain number and waited for him to answer.

"Hey sweetheart ow you?" Rajae said. He was my father's best friend from way back. They started out in this business together and retired together. I asked Rajae why he didn't have any children or never got married. He told me that the one he loved got away.

"I'm good, Parrain. We need you at the house, though. Some more shit jumped off at the states. Eliria sent a couple of people over here to kidnap me so that she can get the Elites on her turf. Poppa is in the shower right now. Once he get out, we are going to go over to one of his old mistress house to ask her about Badrik." I told him.

"Mi pon mi way." He said and hung up.

"Why would Eliria want it with us the way she do? We haven't been moving like we used to in years. What do she really want?" Kymel asked.

"I don't know, but her sending those weak muthafuckers over here, showed us that she really don't know who she is fucking with. I know that they heard of Poppa and my Parrain in their younger days. What makes them think that he was going to let them come in here and take me?" I said.

Kymani hunched his shoulder. "I don't know, man. We gotta get to Badrik's mama house. Poppa had all the fun taking out the entire crew with the twins help. I need to let off some steam."

"What about the woman that you were seeing before you left to go to the states? Y'all looking serious." I asked him.

"We are. I just don't think I am ready to settle down completely. I want to wait 'til I get all the hoe out of me before taking that big step." Kymani replied.

"Why are you two so afraid of commitment? Don't you think that you two are getting too old for all this bed hopping and shit? You do understand that tomorrow is not promised to any of us." I told him and stood up to walk to the window. I wanted my brothers with a stable life with wives and kids.

"Nah, I am not ready for that right now." Kymani said.

"Me either. I be ready to kill muthafuckers over my niece and nephew if someone looks at them wrong." Kymel said. "Besides, I killed a lot of peoples. I don't want people using them as an advantage. I don't understand how you and Jason do it."

"Trust me it is hard being a parent in this business." I told them. Poppa came walking out with another suit on.

"What are y'all talking about in here?" He asked.

"Parenting and being a killer. How did you do it?" I asked him.

"It was easy with you guys because you knew what I did. I didn't hide what I did for a living from you or your mothers. They disagreed, but in the end, you guys were ready to be exactly like me. I took y'all on jobs and let y'all watch what I did. The three of you were fascinated with what I did. I put y'all on and we been tight like this for years." He said. "Did you call Rajae?" Poppa turned to me and asked.

"Yes. He said that he was on his way." I told him. Poppa nodded and walked towards the bar. My father wasn't a drinker like that. He usually had company over that drank a lot. I guess Eliria got his nerves bad. My father's cell phone began to ring. He pulled it out and showed us the screen. It was a private number that my father didn't usually answer. He let it rang until it stopped and started up again.

Poppa put it on silent and sat it on the bar. My Parrain walked in dressed for war. He had on his all black with an AK-47 and a big ass revolver. He didn't play behind his Goddaughter. "Weh di muthafuckas at?" He asked. Poppa almost spat out his good Cognac looking at Rajae.

"Calm your ass down. Winston let you pass with that shit in your hand?" My father walked over with his hand out for the revolver. Rajae handed it to him and leaned the AK-47 against the wall.

"Wah di fuck did him a guh tell me? No. Mi wish dat nigga wud. Mi wudda shot up dat likkle funky ass shack." Rajae replied. No one was going to tell him no to anything. Especially while he was carrying them two big ass guns.

"They you go talking that shit." Poppa said and held the revolver up. "Where the fuck did you get this bitch from." Poppa asked.

"Travis get it fi mi." Parrain answered and then turned around to face me and my brothers. "Waah dis new shit mi hear?"

Poppa passed him his gun back and walked over to the sectional. "Abigay's boy is after Joel. He wants her for himself so that he can be a part of our franchise. He also linked up with some of Jason military buddies and blew up the Center. Eliria stupid ass sent some men here to take Joel. We talked to the last survivor and got all the information from him. We were about to go to Abigay's house to see what Badrick has been doing before he met with his new friends." Poppa told him.

"Let mi check wid mi connects. Eff him dumb ass been moving mi hasn't been quietly." Rajae said. He glanced over at me and winked. "You gave them hell." He asked in perfect English.

"No. Poppa wanted to have some fun alone. The twins helped but Poppa did the damn thing Parrain."

"Girl you don't have to tell me. I was there when your father made Capri swallow his own gun." Parrain said looking back at Poppa. Kymani and Kymel was talking in the corner by themselves. Poppa looked over at them and waited for them to finish. Kymel walked over to Poppa and spoke.

"Yeah Pops. We will stay here and watch over the children and the women. You and El go visit Ms. Abigay." Kymel said. Kymani nodded his head in agreement. Poppa looked over at me and smiled. "I know you game." He told me.

"For whatever." I said to him and jumped up. I kissed my Parrain and walked out the door with my father.

3

JORDAN

We were waiting on Marquel and Malik to arrive at the palace that my brother built. The place also had a cafeteria for the single parents that worked late and couldn't get home in time to cook for their children. Jason said that he wasn't looking to make a profit on that apartment complex because the ones that he had in the other part of the city, was making enough.

I was leaving my apartment to go downstairs to the lobby. Lily called me to check in when they pulled up to the Bailey's resident. I haven't talked to them since, but knew that they needed rest. Especially with being woken up in the middle of the night and breastfeeding Jerimiah. I pulled out my phone and looked at the picture that JoJo put as my wallpaper. JoJo was holding Jerimiah as he slept. The look in his eyes was understandable. He was going to protect him with his life, if need be. It was the same look in my eyes when I was younger watching over Jason and Joseph.

I jumped on the elevator and pressed the button to go down. The door was closing, when I heard someone yell for me to hold the door open. I pressed the button to keep the door open and watched Tank and Tristan come in.

"Dude, I don't know who the fuck this nigga contractors are, but he is going to have to slide that number this way. That shit look better than my house." Tank said.

"Fa real." Tristan agreed.

"Are you getting anything from Marquel?" I asked Tank.

"Fucking right. I got a list of shit I need for this war, fool. I ain't fucking around." He replied and pulled out his list. Tank started naming all types of shit that I knew that he didn't need. The door opened and everybody was already standing at the table looking down at all the shit that Marquel and Malik had laid out. Jason was looking at some more blades. JJ had a Benelli Black Eagle in his hand. It was an autoloading shotgun. That bitch looked bad. I was going to grab one of those and two more Glock 17's.

"Did y'all find them fools yet or not?" Marquel asked.

"Yeah, we got some leads. Tyja pinpointed there main location. I am waiting on some more information from Joel and her brothers. They found out that one of the guys is the son of Callum's ex. Once we get the info we need we will move out." Jason told him.

"Good, because we ready for whatever, Man." Malik said while sitting on the end of the table. It was good to have more men on our side. Jason pulled out his ringing phone and answered it. "Yo."

Jason looked over at Marquel and Malik. "Yeah, let him through." He said and hung up.

"Who was that?" I asked. He shook his head and smiled. I didn't know what the fuck that meant. Everyone else was putting in their order, when a tall ass man walked through the door. He was dark skinned, medium built with a bald head and a box beard. He was wearing a collar shirt and some slacks. The dude looked like he was a salesman.

"Pops, what are you doing here?" Malik asked. Marquel head popped up and he released a sigh.

"You already know why I'm here, Malik. Don't play stupid. I didn't raised you to act that way." The man said. His voice was deep and held authority. I looked at both Malik and Marquel to see if they favor the man that Malik called Pops. They didn't look shit alike.

"Mr. Don Washington, how are you?" Jason said, putting us all out of our misery. Don looked over at Jason and smiled.

"I'm good, Jason. I have been hearing a lot about you and your family. You guys are the ones to fear I heard. Your father would be proud at the things that you guys are doing for yourselves. How is your mother?" He asked.

"She is doing well. She is in Jamaica with my fiancé and her family." He told him. We all looked at him shocked.

"When did that happen?" JJ asked.

Jason smirked at her. "Mind yo business, Bruh." He told him. Don looked over at Marquel with a stern look.

"I know that you want to seek revenge for your cousin and I understand that. But what you need to do is think before acting. We are already under the fucking microscope. Don't do extra shit that they could use against us in the trial." He turned and looked at Malik. "You are our fucking attorney. Why would you think that this shit is ok? I didn't pay for you to go to college and waste your fucking talent on other people shit. You are helping them now by giving them the heat that they need to take care of business."

"That was my family Don." Marquel told him.

"Then give this shit to them for free for handling your lighweight. You know the shit is going to get done. Let them take care of it and you take care of them. Be smart about this situation. If they get you with a body on your name, yo ass is going to jail. And what would happen to Cherrie." Don told him. He was right. The men that killed his cousin was going to die regardless. Marquel wanted to say something but he also knew that Don was right. Jason walked up to him and placed his hand on Marquel's shoulder.

"You know I got you, Bruh. I'll send you the receipts." He told him. Marquel looked up and nodded.

"Good looking out." He said and dapped Jason off. "Whatever y'all need is on the house? If y'all need anything else, let me know and I will get it to you." Marquel said. Don shook his head and motioned for them to leave.

"We got court in a couple of days. Let's get my children together and do dinner." He told them and walked out the door. Malik picked up a duffle bag and tossed it to JJ. "Come get the rest of the stuff out the van." He told him and walked out with Marquel. Tank went with him. I picked up another gun when my phone started ringing.

"Hello."

"Hello. Can I speak to Jordan Davis, please?" A man said on the other line.

"This is he, who is this?" I asked. Jason walked over to me to see what was going on.

"This is Lieutenant Franks of the PFD. We are here at your dealership. It looked like it has been set on fire." Franks said.

"What the fuck did you just say?" I said in an angry whisper. I picked up the remote and turned on the television. I was watching my place of business and cars on fire.

"Your dealership, sir, is up into flames. It has been like that for an hour. The alarms didn't come on, so it didn't alert anyone. We tried to put out the fire but when we spread water on it, it spread more. Someone used some kind of chemical that reacts to water in a violent way. We need you to come down here as soon as possible, Sir." He told me.

"I will send my lawyer there. I am out of the country at the time." I told him and hung up. We knew that they were going to attack, but I didn't know that those muthafuckers was coming like this. In order for him to make do on his promise, he was going to have to burn everything in Philly. We owned, or had our hand in, all businesses around the state. I count that business as a loss but knew that the comeback was going to be real.

JJ ran back into the lobby on his phone. He snatched the remote out of my hand and changed the channel. D1 was also in flames. Firemen and trucks were outside his building, watching the flames die down. "Sir, I can't make it down there at this time. I am out of town on business. I will send someone in my place." He told the man on the phone and hung up. We knew that they were waiting for us to show up. We had to stay back and make sure all of our shit was in order before we met up with them. Matthews was clever to use chemicals to set the fire. That meant that he was more organized than we thought he was.

"We already know who did the shit. There is no need to look at the footage from both businesses. Let's clap back on these muthafuckers. If we can't get to them, let's move in on their family." I said.

Jason nodded his head and picked up his phone. JJ was pissed. I walked over to him and he was in a daze. That club was his baby. It was devastating watching something you built get destroyed. "What!" Jason yelled. "I am on my fucking way, Joel. You got me fucked up if you think that I am going to stay down here." He told her. He listened to whatever she was saying but was set on what he wanted her to do. "After you come from that lady house, make your way back here. There is enough room for everybody. Don't make me come and get you Joel." He said and hung up. This nigga grabbed the table and started breathing heavily.

"J, what's up? Is everyone alright?" I asked. I knew if it was something major, Lily would have called me.

"They sent muthafuckers to kidnap Joel." He mumbled. I looked at JJ and his stupid ass started laughing.

"They tried to kidnap Joel? Gage, nigga. They must have sent the Terminator or Neo from the fucking *Matrix* to snatch her ass up." He said through more laughter. It was something that he needed after seeing his shit burn to the ground.

"She told me that it was some amateurs. Her father took care of them, but that wasn't the point. That hoe ass nigga wants Joel." He said. He was squeezing the table so hard that his knuckles was white. "Call Tyja down here. We are about to move on these muthafuckers." Jason said. JJ pulled out his phone to call her.

"Hey come downstairs. We are ready to move." He told her. Whatever was her response, it had JJ looking at the phone like it was crazy.

"Nobody ain't got time for that. Bring yo laptop and the rest of your shit down here. Don't get fucked up." He yelled at her. "Hello. Hello. I know this muthafucking girl didn't hang up in my face." JJ said and tried calling her back. Her phone went straight to voicemail.

"What did she say?" Tristan asked.

"She said Joel told her not to give us shit and wait for them to get back." He spat. Jason flipped the fucking table over and threw his phone to the wall. He turned and pointed his finger at Tristan. "Go and get your shit." Tristan ran towards the elevator. I was ready to bust some heads like the rest of them. But to see that these fools had their shit in order, we couldn't be out here half stepping. The whole kidnapping Joel sounded strange. Why would they send some bitches that couldn't get the job right? I sat down in one of the chairs and tried to come up with what I would do if I was in charge of their group. And then it came to me.

"I think that we should listen to Joel and wait for them to come back." I said. Jason turned and was ready to swing on me for making that statement. JJ looked over at me.

"Why wait Jo? These niggas are out here tearing up our shit and trying to kidnap El. We should get at those niggas right now."

"Shut up, JJ, and think." I told him. "They sent some weak ass niggas to kidnap Callum's daughter. The man that was over the most dangerous set of assassins. Then you blow up two of our businesses, trying to get a visual on us, so that we could be followed or kidnapped ourselves. Once that shit didn't work, they knew that Jason was going to go after them when he found out about the kidnapping. I believe that made it easy for Tyja and Tristan to find them. They are waiting and ready for us to show up. We don't know if the other assassins are there and waiting, too. We will be out numbered." I told them.

Jason was staring at me. He knew what I was saying was right. He closed his eyes and walked back to his broke phone and picked up the memory card that fell out of it. "Tell Tristan to hold off." He said and walked out of the lobby. Tank walked in with two duffle bags full of extra hardware. I wasn't going to let nobody play with my family. It was time that I took charge and start thinking about what was right for the family.

"Why didn't they show up?" Badrik asked me.

"I didn't think that they were going to show up. Jason and his brothers are very smart men. One of them found out what we were doing. We will have to move on to plan b." I told him. Roc and Geronimo knew each plan that I had laid out of the Davis crew. The others were following our lead. Badrik had his own agenda. I told him that he could have Jason's girl. In the end, I was going to kill her too. She was the reason why my sister died.

Sierra didn't know that Callum was Joel's father. When she put the hit out on her, Callum turned the tables and put the hit out on Sierra instead. My stupid ass brothers and father wasn't shit. They thought that they could go around doing shit to people and didn't think that it was going to backfire on them.

I was the oldest out of the four. My father, Leon, was messing with two women at one time. His wife, whose name was Debbie Ann, was a sweet woman. She was my brothers and sister's mother. They had been trying to have children but was unsuccessful a few times. Leon went to a bar and met my mom, who was a waitress at the time. Leon started throwing money around and told her that she didn't have to work. He told her that he was going to take care of her. My mother didn't believe him at first and ignored his advances, but kept fucking him. My mom missed some days at work, when she found out that she was pregnant. She told my father and he was thrilled.

He told my mom that he was going to leave his wife and move in with her. My mother thought that he would do that. The next day she quit her job and stayed at home. Leon was there for the pregnancy and the birth. Everything looked like it was going my mother's way until Leon's wife got pregnant. My mother was fierce, when he told her that it was a chance that he was the father. They got into a big fight, which caused him to leave.

Leon didn't come back for months. My mother went to the house that he was sharing with his wife, to confront him. Ms. Debbie asked Leon if the baby that my mother was carrying was his or not. He denied everything that my mother said and slammed the door in our face. Mom went downhill from there. She started drinking, doing drugs, and fucking random niggas. As I got older, Mom got worse. It was many of times that I had to pull niggas off her. They would beat her for stealing from them.

The last time I saw Mom was the day that she agreed to let her crack head boyfriend in my room while I was sleep. Sad part about the situation, he wasn't trying to be discrete. He stood over my bed naked and yanked the covers from my body. It was the last week of November and we didn't have heat. I was freezing and reached for the covers. He punched me in the face and turned me on my stomach. He pulled my pants down and tried his hardest to rape me, but my will to kill him was stronger.

I mustered up all the strength and bucked him off of me. He fell backwards on the floor. I picked up the lamp that was by my bed and started smashing it over his head. The lamp was made up of stone, so his head was opened before the lamp broke.

Mom ran in there crying and told me to get out of her house. I was twelve at the time and didn't have anywhere to go. I hopped from shelters to homes and sometimes I stayed on the street for months. I was standing on the corner begging for money, when a woman pulled up in a Lexus Jeep. She rolled down her window and stared at me. She had a boy sitting in the front and the back seat of the car. She looked at her sons and then back at me.

"What is your name?" She asked me. I didn't answer her at first because I didn't trust too many people. I stole and fought to eat.

She continued to wait for my answer. The lady shook her head and pulled out a hundred dollar bill. My eyes got big but I didn't get happy at all. I knew that nothing in life was for free. I stared at her and waited for her to tell me what I had to do for the money.

"All you have to do is tell me your name and you can have this." She told me.

I took a step towards her car and looked at the other boys that were in the car. They were staring at me too with the same color eyes, hair, and face. My shit was dirty, though. I looked back at the woman. "You tell me your name first." I told her.

"My name is Debbie Ann. And you are?" She asked again.

"My name is Levy Matthews." I told her. My father didn't want me with his last name at the time. He told Mom that he wanted us both with it after he divorce his wife.

"Is your mother name, Yvonne?" She asked me. I nodded my head yes. She gave me the hundred dollar bill and smiled. "Where are you staying?" She asked.

"I'll tell you, if you give me another hundred." I told her.

"How about I put you into a nice hotel, where you could get clean and eat whatever you want? Would you like that?" She said.

"I am not going to be your slave, woman." I told her. There was a lot of shit going on in the streets. Some people picked up runaways and have them sleeping in the basement, while working as maids and doing other shit.

"I will never do anything like that to you. I will pay for your hotel room, 'til I find something permanent for you." She said. I didn't want to give in so easily, but it was around winter time and it got real cold at night. I agreed to meet her at the hotel. I wasn't going to jump in the car with her and her two children.

I stayed in the hotel for a week. Ms. Debbie came and picked me up and took me shopping for clothes and food. I thought she was preparing me to go back on the streets. When she pulled over to an apartment building, she told me that I was going to be staying there by myself. I didn't mind that at all because I was already on my own. She walked me to my apartment and gave me the keys. It was a two bedroom, two baths, living space and a kitchen. It was nothing big but it was just right for a twelve-year-old. She brought in a computer and told me that I was to take classes on it. I had online teachers and sometimes when I couldn't figure the shit out, tutors came to me. I stayed in the apartment for four years.

Ms. Debbie would pop up every now and then with her sons and daughter. Brandon and Alan would sometime sleep over and talked to me about their father. I wasn't surprised that they had money. I saw the bills to the place and Ms. Debbie was paying for it out of a savings account that her husband didn't know nothing about. Ms. Debbie dropped Sierra off one day, because she had to go to a doctor's appointment. We sat and talked about everything. She was nine and was getting picked on by an older boy at her school. I told her not to worry about it and that I was going to take care of it. The next day, I went to Sierra's school and beat the shit out the kid. He didn't have a chance. Sierra saw me and ran up to me to give me a hug. She told everyone that I was her big brother. I didn't correct her because that was what she felt like to me.

Ms. Debbie stopped coming around. I called to check on her and didn't get an answer. I called Brandon and he told me that Ms. Debbie was in the hospital. She was sick with cancer. I went to the hospital to see her and that was when she told me the truth. She told me that her husband was my father. I wasn't sure how I felt about that shit. I was happy that she helped build a relationship with my brothers and sister, but she never told my father about me. I told her to get some rest and pulled the covers up to her chest. She reached up and pulled me in for a hug.

"I love you, Levy." She whispered. I looked down at her, hearing those words from a women's lips for the first time. I kissed her on the cheek and walked towards the door. The door opened with the rest of the family walking in. Sierra ran to me and gave me a hug.

"Levy, are you ok?" She asked me.

"I'm good CiCi. I wished I would have known sooner about Ms. Debbie." I told her while looking up into her husband's eyes. He stared at me like he saw a ghost. I didn't linger. I dapped off my brothers and walked out the room. My father came to the apartment later on that night and kicked me out of the apartment. He told me that he wasn't going to hand me nothing for free. I packed some clothes and food. I didn't know how long I was going to be on the streets that time. The difference between the first time being on the streets and this one, I was smarter. I was able to talk my way out of trouble.

The muscle from one of the largest families in the west named

Stephen had been asking around for me. He watched how I carried myself in the streets and brought me on. Stephen gave me money and a cell phone. I called and kept in contact with CiCi. He taught me how to fight and kill when it was necessary, but killing became addictive. I wanted to kill all the time. I had got some orders to kill the first born son of the gun carrier. It was the job that was going to secure my spot on the team of the family. I walked in the restaurant to get an eye on my target and saw that it was Brandon. I turned around and walked out. Stephen approached me and asked why I didn't do the job. I ignored him and kept walking. He came up behind me and placed a gun to the back of my head.

"Go in there and get the fucking job done or I will blow your fucking head off right here, lil nigga." He told me. I reacted too quickly for his eyes. I ducked, grabbed his arm and punched his elbow. He dropped the gun and I grabbed his throat and yanked out his throat. His body dropped before me. And for some reason, that kill made me feel something that I have never felt before. I felt like I was jumping out of an airplane or on the highest rollercoaster ride. I took power from a powerful man. Brandon and his date walked out of the restaurant and turned my way. He saw the body on the ground and nodded his head my way. I didn't know if he knew what was going on, but I didn't stay long to ask. I wanted to feel that feeling again, without getting caught or put in jail. That was why I joined the military. They killed muthafuckers every day.

"Ay, so what's plan b?" Badrik took me out of my thoughts.

"We take out more of their businesses. I will make contact with Davis in a day or two. He will get tired of this cat and mouse shit. We will set up a place where we all can meet up and fight head on." I said.

"Why can't we just do that right now?" Jonathan asked.

"Because, Jason alone will kill the three of you without blinking. We are not ready." Roc told him.

"Fuck that! We are ready. That bitch is the reason why my father rotted his self away in jail. I have been waiting for this moment my whole life. I am tired of playing this sick ass game with him." Luis lashed out.

I kept my head down and tried to calm myself. This was one of the reasons why I didn't like working with groups of people. I had to deal with too many personalities. One wanted to go left and the other wanted to go right. I didn't have the patience or the mindset to deal with shit like this. That was why I always ended up killing the people in my group or the leader of it. Jonathan walked up and stood over me.

"Your plan didn't work the first time, nigga. We need to make the move now." He told me.

I was already pissed that this asshole was standing in front of me, telling me what I needed to do. I stood up with my knife in my hand. I sliced his stomach up from his neck with one swift motion. His breathing started skipping and his head dropped back. I walked away from him and approached the other two.

"We move when I say we move. If you don't like it, you can always take the exit." I told them and pointed to Jonathan who was now trying to close his stomach back up. Geronimo was never the one to watch someone suffer. He pulled out his gun and shot him in the head. Luis and Badrik backed up, and didn't say anything else that night. That was the way I wanted it. Now that we all had an understanding, it was time to move on with the next plan. I picked up the phone and made the call that was going to ravel the empire.

4

JOEL

Poppa and I was on our way to Abigay's home. She stayed on the outskirt of the island, near the water. Poppa told me of their situationship. She was another one that couldn't let go. I didn't understand why my father fucked with women that didn't have they mind together. Kymel told me that their mother was crazy as hell. She tried to kill my father many of times because of his infidelity. She almost did it, if it wasn't for Kymani warning my father of the poison that she put in his food.

Poppa left her that night. Mel and Mani went to stay by Poppa after their mom tried to kill them for looking so much like Poppa. They haven't seen her again after that. Her mother contacted Poppa and told them that they found her body in the house that they used to live in. Kymani and Kymel asked their father to avenge her death. Poppa told them that he was going to look into it, but didn't find out anything. That was strange to me, knowing how well-connected my father was. He could had been found out who did it.

We pulled up to Abigail's home. It looked like the cast from *Property Brothers* came to fix that shit up. It was like walking in the hood and seeing all the fucked up shotgun houses. They all had the same amount of rooms and yard space. You sometimes got that one house that stood out. They had the money to move anywhere else, but decided to stick it out where they grew up. This was one of those times. There were shacks surrounding Abigail's two-story gated home. The house was beautiful. It was green, with a beautiful garden surrounding the house. There was concrete that led to the back, where the basketball court was. The house didn't have a porch, but it sat up off the ground. Poppa parked outside the gate. He got out of the car and pressed the call button. He waited until one of the guards came walking over to the gate.

"Mi here to si Albigay." Poppa told the man.

"Yuh nuh welcome here Callum. Tun an get from round here." The guard told my father and was about to turn his back. Poppa let out a sinister laugh. One thing that Poppa hated was to have muthafuckers turned their back on him, while he was talking with them. He said that was disrespectful on many levels. He did too much for the people here to get the back of an ungrateful bitch.

"Yuh knowing who mi wi ongle mek it worse fi yuh wen mi get mi hands pon yuh." Poppa told him. The guard had fear in his eyes but he was standing his ground.

"Callum wah a pleasant surprise. Wah mi cya duh fi yuh?" Abigail's voice came through the intercom.

"Open dis fucking gate." He said and walked back to the car.

The gate opened and the guard that greeted my father was nowhere to be found. There were other men that was on the property and that followed our car as we pulled in. I counted twelve surrounding the house. That was going to be nothing to take care of. Poppa pulled up in front of the house. A woman walked out with two other men. She was dressed in a dashiki dress with her dreads pulled back. Poppa got out of the car and walked around to open my door. I stepped out with my eyes on the woman. I had my hair slicked down into a bun. I mimicked Poppa and wore a cream, fitted pants suit with no top underneath my jacket. My red pumps and diamond stud earrings completed the suit. My father's suit was black as always but had white trimming around it. You would have thought that we were going to a business meeting.

"I see that you age like fine wine, Callum." She addressed him and was about to lean in for a hug. My father took a step back and pulled me forward.

"Mi neva fi yuh bullshit. Wi need fi chat." He said and motioned for her to lead the way. Her two guards were staring my father down but didn't notice the glare that I was giving them. Abigail turned and walked into her home, with the guards following her. She led us and made a right into a room that had a long table in it. I assume it was for dinners or meetings that her son has. She sat with her back towards the window with her guards. Poppa pulled the chair out and waited for me to sit. He sat next to me and began to grill Abigail.

"Waah yuh bowy up to?" He flat out and asked. Abigail sat back in her seat and held her hand up. The guard placed a cigarette in her hand and the other one lit it.

"Wah it to yuh Callum?" She said and blew smoke out of her mouth. She looked at him and shook her head. "Wah? Wah yuh afraid of a likkle competition?"

"Yuh son nuh pose no threat here Abigail an yuh kno dat. Yuh kno dat eff mi want Badrik dead, it wudda been a lang time ago. Di ongle reason why mi here outta di respect of yuh fada. Tell Badrik to fall back or mi wi forget who grandfatha." He told her. I knew she wanted to come over that table at my father. He didn't leave room for discussion anyway. She smashed her cigarette in the ashtray and looked over at me.

"Did you know that your father used to work for mine?" She said with a smirk. "Your father is the man he is because of the clout that my father had around these parts. He did work for him here and there. We was supposed to run this together. But, he fucked around and got with that crazy ass Vea. He didn't want to believe what he was hearing. You see, he wanted to check things out for his self. He got her pregnant and tried to make her into this wife that he had envisioned." She said with hurt and anger. "And then to add insult to injury, after fucking me, he went to the states and fucked your mother and got her pregnant." She looked at my father with tears falling.

"Mi cud ave been dat uhman to birth all of yuh pickney. Yuh wouldn't ave had fi guh far fi di comfort dat yuh did looking fi. Di peace dat yuh need." She mumbled. Yep, you learned something new every day. I didn't know that Abigail was the daughter of father's boss, Delroy.

"You say that you could have been the one, but you were the first out of the three. I didn't find what I was looking for in you so I moved on. You was there to fuck, true. But that was all that you were good for. Vea was crazy and she was the woman I chose to have my children. If I left you to be with a crazy nutty woman, what does that say about you? Your father knew what type of woman you were and told me not to fuck with you. I was young and dumb at the time and didn't listen. You started showing your ways. You put yourself over others as if you were the queen or some shit. You looked down on the people that helped your father get to where he was. I didn't want or needed selfish bitch by my side. I needed a woman. And you weren't her. You will never be her." My father said in a monotone.

He wasn't affected by the tears that she was spilling while he was talking. He saw what she was trying to do. Hell we both did. Their history wasn't going to save her son and if she kept talking that shit, she wasn't going to make it to bury him.

Abigail slammed her fist on the table and yelled at Poppa. "Fuck Vea! Why wud mi wa fi be dat crazy bitch?" Poppa tilted his head to the side. That was another thing that Poppa didn't tolerate. He hated being yelled at. He took in a deep breath and tried to control his self. He stared at her and replied to her statement.

"Vea didn't have my heart, Abigail." He whispered.

That was new as well. I always thought that Poppa loved my brother's mother. I knew he loved her for giving birth to his sons. But the happily ever after love was what I thought he had with her and it wasn't. The whole time he wished that it was my mother that he could have been with. I wanted to reach over and give him a big hug.

"Oh yeah, your precious Cassidy." She spat out. I couldn't help my facial expression and body language. My mother was a sore spot to me. No one brought her name up unless it was to say something sweet and kind. I knew that this bitter bitch wasn't going to follow that protocol. I readied myself to yank her ass out that chair.

"Be careful Abigail. Watch yuh words inna front of mi dawta." Poppa's voice dropped a few octaves and the temperature in the room changed. Poppa was not visible at the moment. This was the Callum that everyone feared. The two guards stepped forward and was ready to protect her from anything. She looked at me and shook her head.

"I could see why he wants you. You look like the power that men have been fighting for." She turned and looked at my father. "Your time is up Callum. It is my son's time to run Jamaica. It is our time to grab what you took from my family. The Dixion's name will rise as the Bailey's name will be erased from this island." She said.

"Di ongle ting dat wi be erased from dis island wi be yuh entire bloodline. Mi wi mek sure of dat." I spoke for the first time. Poppa sat back and watched the guards. My voice was cold and sharp. They didn't know if they was to protect her from me or Poppa.

"Likkle gyal," she began. I interrupted her by sitting forward with my hands on the table.

"Far from likkle." I said. I stared her in the eyes and saw that fear that me and my brothers feed off of. I felt my hand twitching. I dropped my head back and inhaled the air. I looked back at her and smiled. "Eff yuh ongle kno." I said. Poppa placed his hand on my shoulder.

"That was your warning. Whatever happens after we leave out this door, will be your fault and your fault alone. Your greed for this power that you seek will cause you the only family that you have left." He told her and stood. "Let's go, Baby Girl." He told me. I stood and kept my eyes on Abigail. She was scared no doubt, but I never could have expected what she was about to say. She stood on unsteady feet and began to lash out.

"You think you are so perfect, Callum. You ain't shit. You don't deserve what you have. The Elites should have been with us. With my family. You used them for your own disposal. Tell me what your sons will think when they find out that you sent Gage to kill their mother." She yelled. I stopped and speared her with a look that stopped her and her guards. Poppa stopped and looked at me. I didn't give what I was feeling away. I wanted to show her that what she said didn't affect me at all, but it did.

"Your days are numbered, Abigail. Cherish them?" I told her and walked out the house to the car. Poppa jumped in the driver seat and pulled out the gate and onto the road. We were silent for five minutes. I was trying to control my breathing but it was hard to breathe period.

I was responsible for the death of my brothers' mother. "Stop the car." I whispered. Poppa pulled over and put the car in park. He had a lot of explaining to do. "Why," I asked.

He let out a sigh and rubbed his face down with his hand. "When Kymani and Kymel came to me, they were hurt. The woman that was supposed to love them tried to kill them. She invited them over to dinner when they were eighteen. They walked into the kitchen and she was holding a gun up. It was pointed directly at them. She let off a few shots and hit Kymel in the shoulder. Kymani picked his brother up while dodging bullets, and brought him to the hospital. I got there and they begged me to let her live. I tried to let it go, I did. But the father in me couldn't let her get away with it. She went up to the hospital and tried to finish Kymel off by dosing him with some poison. Kymani stopped her and asked why she was trying to kill them. She told them that she hated me and everything that involved me.

My sons being a split image of myself drove her to hate them too. I couldn't have her living and plotting on my children. I promised them that I wasn't going to put my hands on her. You was my next best thing." He explained. I wasn't mad that I killed her. Mainly with her trying to kill my brothers. I was pissed that he didn't let me know that it was her that I was killing.

"You know that I'm going to tell my brothers. I don't want them to hear this from someone else." I told him. He nodded his head and started the car back up.

My brothers loved their mother and all her flaws. It was hard to explain how crazy a mother was to some devoted ass sons. "Yeah, mi kno." Poppa said and put the car back in drive. We drove up to our home twenty minutes later. Poppa grabbed my hand and squeezed it.

"I'm sorry that I involved you." He said. I shook my head before responding.

"It's ok, Poppa." I said with a smile.

"It's not, Butterfly. I will tell them that it was someone else that killed her. I don't want you guys fighting or trying to kill each other. I will take the heat for all of this if I have to."

"No you won't Poppa. I don't agree with what you did, but I understand. You will not go through this by yourself. I got your back." I told him.

He nodded and got out of the car to open my door. "Let me change clothes first." I told him and ran upstairs. The family was out in the backyard near the pool. Madison and Mason were training with Kymani, while Kymel was in the pool with JoJo. I loved how they treated him. They tried to get Lily to change her mind about him training. She told them that she would think about it when he gets older. I threw on a bra, tank top, some tights, and tennis shoes. I saw Poppa walk out the back to them. I rushed downstairs and saw my brothers walking back in.

"Did you find out anything useful at Abigail's?" Kymel asked, while drying his hair. Poppa walked up behind.

"Get dress and meet us in the office." He said and walked into his office. Kymel looked over at me.

"Is it bad?" He asked. I nodded my head and followed Poppa. Kymani sat in front of the desk watching Poppa. He knew that something was wrong because Poppa look disheveled. Kymel walked in the room putting his shirt on.

"What's going on?" Kymel asked.

I stood behind Poppa. "Badrik is planning on taking over Jamaica. He knows that he will have to get rid of us to that. That was why he linked up with Matthews and the other assassins. He needs help taking us out. He won't be able to do that by his self." I told them.

"Ok, but that is nothing to worry about. We can take care of that. What is really going on, Pops?" Kymani asked.

Poppa took in a deep breath before speaking. "When you was in the hospital Mel, after your mother shot you. I told you guys that I wouldn't harm your mother. I tried. But when she tried to take your life again, I couldn't let her live." He told them. Kymel and Kymani's body language and demeanor changed. Kymel walked up to the desk and stood next to Kymani.

"Yuh had sup'm fi duh wid mi mada death?" Kymel asked. Poppa nodded. Kymani stood up next to Kymel. I saw what they were planning in their eyes. But, I wasn't going to let it go down like that. I came around Poppa seat and stood next to him. "Yuh fucking lied to fi wi face wen wi ask yuh eff yuh kno nuhting bout it! Di man dat teach wi dat liars cyaa be trust!" Kymani yelled.

"Mi did wah necessary as a fucking fada! Yuh mada did full of hate an grief. Eff mi wudda let har live shi wudda keep trying til shi succeeded. It dida mi job to protect yuh. Mi wudda radda live wid har death dan di death of mi sons." Poppa told them.

"Eff dat did wah it did why lie. Why nuh tell wi di truth an wi wudda dealt wid it den." Kymel asked with his anger boiling. He was trying to hold back, but I could see that he was about to explode.

"No yuh wouldn't ave dealt wid Kymel. Yuh wudda lashed out an guh afta di one mi send to kill har an dat did sup'm dat mi cud nuh let yuh duh." He said. Kymel and Kymani eyebrows went up. Kymani let out an evil laugh, as Kymel gave us a sinister smile.

"Who yuh did trying to protect father? Dat person worth more to yuh dan di relationship wid yuh sons cuz mi guarantee dat person dead whetha yuh wa dem to be or nuh." Kymel said. That had Poppa standing up. He knew that they were going to come after him and he was ok with that. But to threaten me, was different. He didn't play that shit even if they didn't know that it was me.

My brothers saw that my father was ready to go to war with them. They forgot that it was this man that taught them everything they knew. My father was still in shape and one of the deadliest men in the world. My brothers were going to lose. Because I wasn't going to let them jump him.

"Who di person dat get yuh feeling young again?" Kymani asked. Poppa stood still and stared them both down.

"Nuh need fi be young again to deal yuh Kymani. Try mi." Poppa ignored his question and began to take off his jacket. Kymel looked over at me and gave me a stern look.

"Stay outta it El dis nuh ave nuhthing fi duh wid yuh." He told me low and deep.

"Sorry bredda, it ave everything to duh wid mi." I told him. They both looked at me curiously.

"El," Poppa scolded.

"I did it." I told them. "I was the one that killed your mother." The look in their eyes had me dropping my bad ass Gage act. They were hurt. I have never saw that look from them. They always had to portray themselves as the big brothers. The ones that you couldn't hurt or tear down. The ones that I could call on if someone fucked with me. I walked around the table to talk to them.

"I heard what happened to you, Mel. If I would have found out, I would have killed your Mom anyway." I told them. They stood there in pain. And for the first time, I couldn't take it away, because I was the cause of it. Kymel's eyes closed and Kymani looked over to Poppa.

"Yuh send mi sista to kill mi mada." Kymani asked him. Poppa kept his eyes on Kymel. Kymel was close to his mother. Kymel opened his black eyes and stared at me with tears running down his face. That shit broke my heart. "Kymel, look at me son." Poppa asked. Kymel wasn't hearing shit that Poppa was saying. His focus was on me. He wasn't calculating his moves the way he would. He was about to attack me out of rage and pain.

"Yuh ave no regrets," Kymel asked me, opening and closing his fist. He flexed his muscles and his breathing picked up. I took a step back and got back into attack mode.

"None," I answered. He moved his neck from side to side and maintained eye contact.

"Neitha mi wi," he said and charged at me. I had enough time to block the first blow but the other landed on the right side of my face. I stumbled back and hit the wall. He kicked his foot out and missed as I dodged it with a blow of my own to his neck. I moved from the wall and got in the middle of the office. Kymel turned and squared off with me. I calmed myself and concentrated on not killing him. I knew he was hurt, but I wasn't going to let him beat his pain away out on me. I blocked his vicious blows, but suffered from them. He was tagging the shit out of my arms. I heard Poppa and Kymani shuffling in the background.

Kymel swung at me again. I blocked that hit with my right and hit him with a strong left punch to the forehead. He went back again, but this time I didn't wait for him to recover. I rushed him hitting all his main points. I was about to deliver my special blow but was picked up and tossed to the other side of the room. Poppa helped me up and stood by my side. Kymani checked on Kymel and turned towards us. My entire face was hurting from the blow that Kymel served me. I threw my arms out to loosen the pain that they were in. Kymani had a busted lip and a small knot forming on the side of his head. Kymel's eye was swollen and almost closing.

"Yuh ave no regrets El. None fi mi feelings or pain!" Kymel yelled at me. Kymani held him back from getting closer.

"That is bullshit and you know it. You are my fucking brother Mel. You think that I was going to let her live after trying to kill you and Mani more than once. She was lucky that Poppa waited two years after you got shot to make that order." I told him and stepped forward. "I do not feed off your pain and misery, brother. I am sad that you are hurting, but I am not sorry for doing what any of you would have done for me."

"Really, yuh ass did bout to kill wi both wen wi did trying to kill Jason yuh protect dat nigga from wi." Kymani fired back.

"Fuck off, Mani. That was different. If Jason would have tried to kill me when I was pregnant with the Lovies, I would have killed him myself. I wouldn't have gave him chances after chances to get the job done, no matter who he was. But, he didn't lay a fucking hand on me or our children. That was a bad fucking example, Nigga. You reaching." I spat at Mani. Whenever he felt like he was losing, he would always through some shit at you that didn't have anything to do with the current situation. That shit pissed me off.

"Dat wuh mi mada, EL." Kymel whispered. I walked all the way to him and pushed Mani big ass out of the way. I placed my hands on his face and stared up into his eyes. I wasn't going to bullshit him, because that was not how our father raised us to be.

"Mi sorry fi yuh pain Bredda. Di grief dat mi wudda feel eff shi wudda taken yuh from mi, wudda make mi crazy. Tell mi wah mi need fi duh to heal yuh broken heart Mel. Mi wi duh nuhting." I told him. He sighed and took my hands off his face. I thought that he was going to pay no attention to what I said. He held my hand and placed them on his heart. He leaned his forehead to mine and closed his eyes.

"Mi need time, Joel. Even though mi mada did crazy, shi did still mi mada. Just gimme sum time to tink things ova." He said and kissed me on my forehead. He took a step back and glanced over to Poppa.

"Mi wudda respect yuh decision cuz mi kno wah type of man dat yuh an ow yuh feel bout yuh pickney. Mi kno dat yuh kno sup'm bout mi mothas death. Mi neva kno dat yuh did involve dis much. Yuh cud ave tell wi." He said to Poppa and walked out the office. Kymani looked at me and grabbed the back of my neck to bump heads.

"Love you," he told me and kissed me on my nose. He went to check on Mel. Poppa walked around his desk and sat. I saw the tiredness in his eyes. It was the same thing that I saw in T Glen eyes. He was getting too old for this shit. He should be somewhere enjoying his grandbabies. Instead, he was battling with old wounds that was going to remain painful, every time he looked into his son's eyes.

"We have to get back to the states and let them know what we found out. Tyja is trying to keep Jason at bay 'til we get there, but they are getting relentless. There is one thing that was bothering me about this situation. How do you think that Abigay got that information? Did you try to hire someone else to do the job?" I asked him. Poppa dropped his head back and stared up into the ceiling fan that was in his office.

"Only two people knew about me sending Gage out to kill Vea. You don't count, because you didn't know who Vea was at the time." Poppa said more to himself.

"Who was the other?" I asked.

5

JASON

I was laying in the bed alone sleeping uncomfortably. Joel and I have been together ever since the shit went down with the Stand's family. I was surprised that I let her and the kids go to Jamaica without me. I was about to get up and watch television. I knew that I wasn't goin' to get any sleep without my family. It was no use in trying. I felt hands rubbing on my leg. I didn't like the whole anticipation thing. I grabbed her arms and pulled her up to my face. She smiled at me with her beautiful brown eyes shining on me. "I told you about them games."

She threw her head back and gave me a sexy giggle. She looked back at me with her bottom lip in between her teeth. "You know how my games end up. Why are you complaining?"

"Because, it feels like it has been forever since I had you." I said and reached down to grab a handful of her thick ass. Her body was soft and smooth as shit. She smelled like vanilla and cocoa butter. Joel knew how much I loved that smell. It drove me fucking crazy. I grabbed her hips and pulled her up some more. She sat up and smiled.

"I thought that you wasn't for all the games." She teased. I smacked her on the ass.

"When it comes to me and my meals, I don't play and you know it. Come have a seat." I told her. She got on her feet in a squatting position and grabbed onto the headboard. Her sweet lips were already juicy with her nectar dripping. I stuck my tongue up and swiped her nub. The moan that came from her lips, encouraged me to latch on and suck for dear life. She tried to escape my tongue by standing. I wasn't going to let her get away that easy. My arms were already under her leg. I grabbed both of her thighs and pulled her down, which made her drop to her knees.

"Oh, baby. Slow down shit." She moaned out

I wasn't slowing shit down. This was what happened when I went without her. I get all savage and possessive. She could've talked that shit too, but she loved it as well. I didn't need to place my finger in her, because my tongue was doing all the work. She began to ride my face and groaned louder. I didn't know if the kids were in the other room. Unlike the rooms at our home, these weren't soundproof. I slapped her on her ass to quiet her down. She looked down, begging me with her eyes to make her come. I knew that baby girl was close, because her leg started shaking.

"I need, J. Please give it to me." She begged out loud. I licked and sucked 'til her ass was in that bitch screaming for me to stop. I didn't want to stop. Her juices were too sweet for me to waste a drop. Her flexible ass fell back and reached for my dick in my boxer briefs. She pulled it out and started massaging it. I quickly pulled away from her nub and hissed like a hoe.

Joel had the magic touch. I was already hard as fuck from the way I had her up in here moaning. But, once her hand started stroking my dick, I was the one moaning all loud and shit. "Fuck, El." I told her. I couldn't take that shit any longer or I was going to bust in her hand. And that was something that I didn't want to do. I grabbed her waist, which had my piece slipping out of her hand. I sat up and hovered her over it. She grabbed my face gently and pulled me into a sweet kiss. The kiss that slowed whatever I was about to do down. She didn't want to fuck tonight. She wanted me to hit her with them long, deep strokes. Slowly.

I was learning, but that shit was pure torture. I hated and loved it at the same time. I felt more than her walls closing in on me when we made love. I felt her heart beat at the same pace as my own. I felt the way she gave herself completely to me, without throwing up her defensive walls. She was open like a book to read. And I always finished the story.

I lowered her down on my piece steady and easy. Her breathing skipped with every inch that she took in. I closed my eyes and tried to concentrate on not pushing inside of her quickly. She rotated her hips 'til she was seated all the way on me. *Fuck*! She started grinding and biting on my neck gently. I didn't know why she did shit like that when she knew how turned on I got. I maintained my strokes and had us both climbing for that new high.

I flipped us over, without breaking connection. I spread her legs open and fell between them. I didn't like missionary at first. It seemed like it was too personal. Sex with a random person was just sex. There were positions that I did with Joel that I would have never done with other women. I didn't like seeing their face or the expressions that they made. I was staring down at Joel and watched how she reacted to me being inside her. She was so responsive to my touch.

Joel wrapped her legs around me and it pulled me in deeper. "Faster, Baby." She whispered. I placed my lips on hers and stared moving in and out faster, the way she liked it. Fuck, it was the way that we both liked it. The bed started rocking and knocking against the wall.

"Oh shit, El. I'm right there. Fuck, I swear I could live in this pussy, girl." I told her and started banging her ass harder. She chanted my name over and over, 'til we both released. I rolled off of her quickly, because I knew that I was ready to drop on her ass.

I guess we were too loud, because my phone began to ring. My ass was out of breath and couldn't move. "Babe, please answer that for me." I said with my eyes still closed. The phone started ringing again, after it stopped. I reached over and tried to slap Joel on her ass, but missed. I opened my eyes and Joel was nowhere in sight. I sat up and looked around the room. My bedroom door was open and there was no other luggage in the room but mine. I dropped back down and closed my eyes. I haven't dreamed about fucking since I was twelve, and here I was laying here with my dick leaking with cum. My phone began to ring again with Joel's ringtone. It was the song that she sang for me at Sincere's club. I picked it up and answered. "I want you so fucking bad right now." I told her, while not giving a fuck if she had me on speaker.

She giggled and let out a sigh. "I want you, too, Baby. But there is a lot that we gotta catch up on. We got some information about Badrik out here that we can use against him." She said. I sat up and heard the hesitation in her voice. Something else was up.

"What's wrong El?" I asked her. The line went quiet for a minute before she responded.

"I'll tell you when I get there. We all are on our way back now. There are some other things that I want to run by you." She told me. She sounded like she hadn't slept at all up there.

"Aight. Bring your ass straight to the apartments, Joel. Don't take any detours nowhere." I said. "I love you." I whispered.

"I love you too. See ya soon." She said and hung up.

I tossed my phone on the bed and got up to take a shower. I knew that it was going to be busy as fuck. I was waiting on my Seal brothers to arrive and a word from Dex. He was probably laying low 'til he knew that they didn't have the drop on him.

After I finished taking care of my hygiene, I went into the living room and turned on the television. Two buildings that my family was affiliated with was burning on the news. The difference between the ones that happened the other day was this one had casualties. Fourteen people were burned alive, trying to get out of the building. Firefighters reported that there were chains on the door, keeping the people in, while the building burned. We were partners with the owners of that building. We didn't think that he would go after them as well. My phone rang again. I walked to the bedroom and picked it up, after lowering the volume on the television.

"Yeah," I answered.

"Are you seeing this shit, Bruh? That was Marlon spot. Matthews also took out Lenny's Barber Shoppe. He had kids in there, Man." Jo said.

I heard that nigga breathing hard through the phone. Those were his business partners. I didn't have any. I didn't want to go into business with no one that wasn't family. Jordan and Joseph was losing a lot and for the first time, the shit was all my fault.

"I see it. I am on my way to the lobby. Meet me there with the rest of the group." I told him and hung up.

I called JJ's phone and he didn't answer at first. I checked the time and saw that it was noon. We have been up all night with Matthews shit. JJ was the type to need rest and food. He was like a pregnant woman sometimes. I tried calling again and this bitch sent me to voicemail. I grabbed my keys and walked out the door. JJ and Tyja was staying next door to my condo. I walked up to his door and knocked on it like I was the police. I heard JJ stumbling to the door and talking shit. He opened the door with a gun in his hand. "What the fuck do you want?" He growled at me.

"Get yo tired ass up. We got work to do. Where is Tyja?" I asked.

"She went downstairs to eat breakfast. What's going on?" He sobered up.

"They hit two more spots." I told him. "Joel and the family is on their way back. They got some information for us. Get dressed and meet me downstairs." I said and turned towards the elevators. I jumped on and checked my messages. I didn't receive any that were important enough for my attention at the moment.

I got to the lobby and saw the family eating, while watching the news. Tyja and Tristan were already on their computers ready for orders. Jo was on the phone talking to the other people that he was in business with. He had to warn them of our situation, so that they could close down 'til further notice. He promised to pay whatever they will lose while they were closed. Tank walked over to me and shook his head. "This is some fucked up shit, Jason. That fool is really fucked up in the head." He told me.

"Shit, you have no idea." I responded and walked over to Tyja. I guess Joel gave her the ok, because she didn't want to come out her room last night. "What else did you find?" I asked Tristan and Tyja.

"Nothing. We have locations on the Jonathan and Luis families." Tristan answered. I shook my head knowing what Matthews was up to. JJ walked over to me with Jo. "What's wrong J?"

"Matthews has always had problems working in a group. Roc and Geronimo don't have nothing to lose. That is why they worked well together. They don't have shit to destroy or go after when they attack people. Matthews will kill the other three or let us kill them off easily. I don't know that bitch Jonathan, but Badrik and Luis has their own agenda and that is not going to work for Matthews. He needs everyone on one accord. His accord." I told them.

"So, if he didn't really need them, why would he bring them on his team?" JJ asked.

"Because, the men have something against us. The more people that hate us, the better for them. Matthews also realized that the Elites are better than the Eliria's Gang. He will try to throw us off with other tactics. It's something that we will have to get prepared for because his main objective is to break this family apart." I told them. Everyone nodded their understanding. My phone beeped letting me know that I had an incoming text message. One from Charlie, letting me know that my two guests arrived and another from someone I didn't know. I ignored it and walked to the door to meet Sincere and Stipes.

I pulled the door open and they were walking towards it with their duffel bags. "I heard on the news about some buildings being destroyed. Was that yo shit?" Sin asked after dapping me off.

"Yeah. It was my big brother business." I answered.

"Do we know if we have eyes on him or the other men?" Stipes asked.

"No we don't have eyes on them, but we do know where they are in the city, held up somewhere." I told them and walked back into the lobby. JJ and Jo approached us first. "These are my brothers, Jordan and Joseph. That is Tank and Tristan, my cousins. And the young lady is Tyja. These are my Seal brothers, Sincere and Ron, but we call him Stipes." I said. They shook hands and told me what Tristan found.

"You was right. They found an unidentified body off the bank. Tristan went into the system and got the fingerprints of the man. It was Jonathan. He was sliced opened and had a gunshot to the face."

"Good, that's one less asshole we gotta worry about." JJ said. Sincere shook his head.

"No, it's bigger than that. He killed Jonathan too early. We was supposed to kill him so that he could blame it on the Davis crew. You guys gotta dig a little deeper to see who Jonathan was close to." He asked.

"The only one that comes up is his brother that teaches at NYU." Tyja answered. Stipes walked over to her and leaned down to see her computer screen.

"What is his brother's name?" Tyja started typing and pulled up Jonathan's brother information.

"His name is Rory Edwards."

"That's not no fucking, Rory Edwards. That's Ahmad Valez. He was the muthafucker that made the poison that killed the Hopkins family last year. He was hired by the government to create more of that special shit but he declined. They took everything from him and put him on the Most Wanted list. I don't know who fixed his shit up that good to get him a job." Stipes said. Tyja started punching on those and pulled the picture of Ahmad on the television screen. He did look familiar. He must have got some work done as well.

"Do you think that they are real brothers?" Jo asked.

"Yes. Matthews probably wanted to work with Ahmad at first. He was trying to stay clean and declined their offer. They let Jonathan on the team, to get him killed. And when that happen, Ahmad would jump at the offer that he dismissed. It's all in Matthews' plan." Sincere said. "What's up, Ty?"

"Hey Sin. Who you let run your club while you out here?" Tyja asked him.

"Honor running it. You know she don't play about my baby." He said with a chuckle.

Honor was Sincere's little sister. The way their relationship was, you would have thought that Honor was older. She made sure that Sin had whatever he needed. She used to send us care packages when we were overseas. Stipes had a thing for her, but she told him that he wasn't mature enough to be with her. I didn't understand how he was ready to put up with her attitude. Every time we saw each other, I wanted to throw her ass out the window. I had to make sure I ate or wasn't too tired to have to take a nap at his place. Honor goofy ass would blast the music or would cook enough for her and Sincere. He thought the shit was funny and didn't tell her nothing about it. His punk ass was scared of her.

"Yeah, Honor be ready to throw everybody out the club." Tyja said and shook her head. The television started beeping and we all looked up. It was a satellite picture of the neighborhood where my mother's house was. Tristan did more clicking and a house was highlighted. It was a yellow single story family home. They had a small yard in front the house.

"What we looking at Tristan?" I asked him.

"I don't know. A window popped up on my laptop. It told me to open it up. I checked for viruses or anything that would lead the sender to our location. It was clean. I clicked on it and this popped up." He said looking up at the screen. We all stared at it and thought that it was nothing, 'til Badrik and Roc came out the side door.

"Find out who name that house is under." I told Tyja. We watched as Tyja got the information. Roc and Geronimo jumped in a car and left. "Tristan, follow them and see where they are going." We watched as the satellite followed them around the city. We didn't know what or where they were going. I was happy that we got the family out the house. I didn't know how long they been staying there or planning these attacks. Madison dealt with Sierra a couple of days ago.

"Abigail Reid is the name of the woman that owns the house. She bought it three months ago. All of the bills are under her name as well. Strange thing about that is she haven't been down here since she bought the house over the phone. She has two other homes. One in Texas and the other one in New Orleans." Tyja said.

"Is she related to anyone on Matthew's team?" JJ asked. Tyja shook her head no. The satellite followed them for hours. Tyja pulled up another feed to watch over the house that they came out of. We saw Badrik past the apartments that we were in. It didn't look like they knew that this where we were. Sin and Stipes got with my brothers to discuss something that they thought they should know about Geronimo and Roc. Night approached us quick and it was still quiet. Matthews didn't come out the house and Badrik was still riding around with Roc. Tyja was about to say something, but Tristan interrupted her.

"They arrived at the airport." I turned my head to the screen and looked at the plane that was landing. My phone rung and I pulled it out of my pocket to answer it.

"El, where are you?" I asked walking closer to the television.

"We just landed. Can you please send someone to the grocery store for some potatoes and shrimps? The kids wanted smothered potatoes. T Glen promised to make a pot big enough for everyone to eat. Did your friends arrive yet?" Joel said.

"Joel, what airport are you at right now." I asked her.

"The private one. Why Jason? What's wrong?" She said with concern. I watched as Roc pulled out his phone.

"Joel," I called out. The plane was landing and coming to a stop. "El baby, please tell me you are not on the landing strip waiting to get off the plane.

"Jason, what is wrong?" Her voice got stern.

Roc held up his phone and pressed the button. In a blink of an eye, the plane blew up on the runway. Joel's phone went dead.

"Joel," I whispered.

"J," Jo walked up to me with caution. "What happened?" I couldn't answer him. I didn't want to until I was sure. I redialed her number and her phone went straight to voicemail. I called everyone's phone that was on that plane and no one answered. My heart dropped and rage like nothing I have ever felt before, rose up in me. My life was on that fucking plane. Everyone that I was living for. My mother. My children. My El. My fucking heart. I watched as Roc and Badrik jumped back into their car, satisfied with their work. I was seeing red. Nothing. But. Red. I crushed my phone.

Without talking to anyone, I walked out of the lobby and to my car. I didn't hear anything that was going on behind me. I didn't want to. I was on my way to the house where those niggas was staying. They all were going to die. I didn't care if I was going to get killed. I was like them now. I didn't have nothing to live for. I peeled off from my parking spot, headed towards the front gate. Charlie had the gate open, waiting on me to exit. I raced out those gates and flew down the streets of Philly. I was pushing ninety in the residential neighborhood. I ran every light and stop sign to get to them niggas.

I wanted to make it there before Roc and Badrik did. I wanted to be waiting at the door for them, while drenched in the blood of those other three assholes. I knew that this was a part of Matthews' plan. I was falling into the trap that was going to seal my fate. I turned right and then had to make a sharp left. I eased off the gas and turned left and straighten out the wheel quick. I kept my speed at an easy pace.

I was four blocks away from the house. I took in a deep breath and was prepared to take fire from Geronimo, who was on the roof somewhere. I was at the end of the fourth block, when a truck appeared out of nowhere. I couldn't stop myself from hitting it. I threw my seatbelt on and braced myself for the impact that my body was about to take. I hit the truck and the airbags burst out. I jammed my shoulder and neck. I dropped my head back and felt my face. It felt like it was on fire. My door opened with someone pulling me out the vehicle. I was disoriented, but still quick. I pulled out my gun to shoot the muthafucker. My gun was knocked out my hand and the person pulled my arm back. I struggled, not making it easy for them.

I heard Sincere wrestling with someone behind me. I knew that he would have been the only crazy one to come after me. Stipes stayed behind to take care of my family, just in case we died. Another body got in front of me. I couldn't make out who it was due to the airbag deploying in my fucking face. Hands were placed on my face, and I could've sworn that it was the hands that I have been craving throughout the night.

"Jason, focus baby. Focus on my voice. It is me. I am here, Luv." I heard her say.

Naw. I couldn't fall for this shit. I yanked from her and tried to get away from the one that was holding me down. She grabbed my face again but held onto it tightly. "It is me, Jason. Look at me, Baby. Look!" She stressed. I heard her take a deep breath in and leaned forward. "You and Mason picked up you and your father's habit. You guys wake up every morning and watch cartoons. You had a debate on which character was the smartest. You picked Road Runner and Mason picked Bugs Bunny. You guys got so loud that Madison tried to reason with you both." She said and rubbed my face again. "It is me, Luv." She finished.

I shook my head and tried to focus on her. My vision was a bit blurry but I saw what I needed to see. Her long curly blonde hair wild and untamed. Her eyes were filled with concern and determination. I inhaled her lavender and cocoa butter smell. How can this fucking be?

"We will explain later. Right now we gotta get the fuck out of here." She said. The man let my arm go and helped me up. I turned and saw that it was Kymel. He looked like he was in a fight. Sincere and Kymani were in a stand-off with their guns pulled.

"Sincere, please don't kill my brother." Joel said and grabbed my arm to guide me to the car. He looked over at her and smiled, but didn't drop his weapon. "It's cool, Sin. They are family." I told him. Kymani dropped his weapon and took a step back. Sin stared him down until he got to the car. Joel placed me in the car and sat next to me. Her brothers jumped in the front seat and pulled off before we were noticed.

6
JOEL

I knew that Jason was going to go off on the deep end doing what I did. We had to make sure that it looked like they killed us, so that they won't be expecting us. I wanted to talk to Jason about this but made the decision on my own to go through with the plan. I shut my phone off after I heard the plane blow up on the other side of the airfield. Abigay must have told Badrik about our meeting. He didn't want to kidnap me now. He wanted me and the rest of my family dead. He didn't know how much he had fucked up. Oh, but he will. Him and his bitch ass mama. I couldn't wait to get my hands on her.

I looked at Jason and saw all the abrasions to his face. He was staring at me as if he would have blinked, I would've disappeared. "Why El?" He asked while caressing my face.

"We had to make sure that we weren't followed? Badrik is trying to take over Jamaica. If he can get all of the Baileys in one spot, he would have taken advantage of it. He tried and failed." I told him.

"You could have warned me, Joel. I lost my fucking mind that quick." He mumbled.

"You was supposed to." Kymani said and kept driving. Kymel sat in the passenger seat quiet and distant. Jason felt how different the atmosphere was. I knew that I needed to tell him about our situation, but it was something that I couldn't do right now. The look on Jason's face said different. Especially when he noticed the bruise on my face. He sat up, disregarding his injuries and grabbed my chin. He tilted upwards and to the side to get a better view of it. I looked in the rearview mirror and saw Kymani staring at us. He knew what Jason was going to do after finding out what Kymel had done.

"What happened to your fucking face, El?" He asked harshly. I tried to remove his hand but he knocked it out of the way. "Don't do that shit, Joel. I asked you a fucking question and I expect you to answer it."

We had enough problems as it was. I didn't need my brother fighting my Luv. "We found out that my father ordered Gage to kill our mother. I hit her. She hit me. And now we are good." Kymel told him. Jason's eyes shot back to mine. I didn't hold my head down or avert my eyes. I did what I did, and didn't give a fuck about how muthafuckers looked at me. I was ready to explain that to Jason, but his eyes didn't hold judgment. He nodded his head and sat back, pulling me with him.

"Where are the kids?" He asked.

"They are at the apartments waiting on you. You would have known that if you would have answered your phone. I emailed Tyja right after my phone disconnected. She said that she was yelling for you, but you didn't hear her. You didn't hear Jo telling you that Lily texted him and told him that we were okay. You must have zoned completely out." I said.

"You have no idea." He answered with his eyes closed. I knew that airbag fucked him up pretty bad. He was going to need rest before we went on attack mode. I didn't need him out here performing at fifty percent, but even at fifty, he could've given anyone a run for their money. I wasn't going to chance it though.

We pulled up to the apartments in record time. Kymel jumped out the car and opened the door for me. He hasn't talked to me since we left Jamaica. I guess that was what he needed. Jason got out the car with no help. Sincere walked over to him and stood by his side just in case he needed it. We met up in front of the truck and grabbed each other's hands. He pulled my hand up to his lips and placed his velvet lips on them.

We followed behind my brothers and went inside to our waiting family. Mason and Madison ran to their father and hugged his leg. Jo was sitting with his sons and Lily on the love seat. Tyja and JJ was standing in front of Ma-Ma, while Tank and Tristan were talking to T Glen. Poppa was in his own little world. He knew something was up but didn't want to tell me yet. Whatever it was had him hurting and pissed at the same time. When he packed to come down here, he stuffed jeans and t-shirts in his suitcase. That was very unusual for him. I was going to ask Kymani or Kymel about it, but they weren't talking to Poppa at all.

"Daddy, what happened to you?" Madison asked him. He kneeled before her and kissed her on the forehead.

"I had a fight with a truck and lost. I'm good now that I see your sweet face." He told her. She smiled at him and wrapped her arms around his neck. The bond that they had was something I couldn't get over. It was fascinating.

"What made you think that you could take on a truck, Dad? That was suicidal." Mason told his dad. Jason looked up at me. I shook my head and placed my hand on his shoulder. I knew he felt that he had nothing to live for after thinking that we were gone. The world would be in a world of trouble if anything happened to us.

"Are you going to introduce us to our niece and nephew?" Sincere asked, while standing behind me. His other friend came forward as well. Jason stood up and grabbed Madison's hand.

"Of course. This sweet little angel is Madison and this is my main man Mason." He said. Stipes stepped forward and grabbed Madison's hand.

"You are beautiful, little one. I am your Uncle Stipes. With a smile like that, you can have anything you want." He said and kissed her hand.

"Hi Uncle Stipes. Do you mean it? Will you give me anything I want?" She asked him. I was afraid of what she was going to ask for.

Lately, Jason has been giving her every weapon she asked for. Stipes nodded his head.

"I saw the Jagdkommando Dagger in your bag. I was waiting for our weapons' expert to find one, but he said that he had to order it. Can I have that please?" Madison asked after batting her long eyelashes. Sincere stood up straight and looked at Jason.

"What the hell have you been training these kids?" He asked. We all shook our head and laughed. Sincere introduced his self to the children and everyone else. Ma-Ma came over to check on Jason and his injuries. We were waiting on one more person before we started handing out information. Ma-Ma and T Glen cooked and fed everyone dinner. Poppa was still standing in the corner by his self. Jason talked with the children as I took care of his wounds.

Two hours later, my Parrain walked in. "Ok Luvies. It's time for y'all to go to bed. Your father and I will be up later." We hugged and kissed them goodnight. Ma-Ma took them up with Lily and her boys. T Glen glared at Tank and Tristan. Tank was the bold one to address her.

"What's wrong Ma?" He asked her. She shook her head with disappointment.

"When am I going to get my grandchildren?" She asked the both of them. Tristan almost fell out of his seat and Tank looked at her wide-eyed.

"You want grandbabies?" Tank asked. T Glen looked at him, like she wasn't going to repeat herself.

"Can we talk about all this when everything is over with?" Tristan asked uncomfortably.

"Why you all nervous and shit? You talking like you don't want me to know that you having sex. I know you fucking Tristan. Why don't you slip up and give me my damn grandchild." T Glen said to him. We tried to hold in our laugh, but T Glen never did care who was in the room when she was ready to speak her mind.

"Have you been drinking?" Tank asked her.

"What type of question is that, when yo dumb ass fixed me two drinks? I ain't drunk. I want my grandbabies. You betta start trying or

I will start recruiting." She said and walked to the elevator cursing her boys out. Tank looked at us with an apologetic look. Tristan's face was so red that you would have thought that T Glen caught him fucking.

"Aight. Now that everyone is here, let's exchange information." Jason said, getting everyone back on board. Sincere and Stipes told us everything that we needed to know about their Seal brothers. We told them what we found out about Badrik, but left everything else out, including us being the Elites. What happened in our family was up for a group discussion. I was going to tell Jason once we got alone. I looked over at my Parrain and waited for him to tell us what he found out.

"Badrik and Luis are working together. Luis had been looking for exotic children. Badrik promised Luis children from Jamaica that could clean, cook, or be used for whatever he wanted them to be. Badrik knows if Callum running the island, he won't be able to deliver. Taking the Bailey's out will be the only way for him to do that. Madison and Mason is a bonus. Luis said that they should live without their father, just like he did. He wants them to suffer." Parrain said.

"And that is where the problem lies. Matthews want my children dead. He will kill Badrik and Luis to make that happen." Jason said.

"Ok, we got them down. What about the Eliria's Gang?" JJ asked.

"The people that they sent were from France. Eliria has her hand in this somewhere. We have to find that angle." I told them.

"Speaking of angles, we are trying to find out if a lady name Abigail Reid is related to any of the men at the house that they are staying in." Tyja said. Poppa stood up with his nose flaring and fist bald.

"Why do you ask?" Poppa said.

"She is the owner of the house." Tyja said.

"I'm on it." My Parrain replied and pulled out his phone. He walked out the door to conduct his business.

"But, this is good. We have the advantage. Matthews thinks that he got rid of your family. He was expecting you to come at him with full force. If you don't react the way he assumed you would, he would have to find another way to grab your attention. Most of your family was on the plane. I'm surprised he didn't try to contact you to see if you know about them or not." Stipes said.

"Can you pull up the surveillance around the house again?" Jason asked. The satellite zoomed in on the house. The lights were out with no movement. Kymani and Kymel walked up to the screen. "Can you rotate it?" Kymani asked.

Tristan rotated it and we saw a car with two men posted in the middle of the next block. It blended in well with the other cars on the street. "That is Badrik and Roc right there. They are waiting on you too." Jo said. Tristan pulled the view back and we didn't see the car that Jason drove. It looked like the accident never happened.

"Where is my car?" Jason sat forward and asked. Kymel walked towards us and answered. "We brought a few men back with us. We had them clean the spot up before anyone would notice. We told them to bring it to Tank's shop on Lincoln Ave."

"Good looking," Jason responded and got up. "I am going to go upstairs and change out of these clothes. Mr. Lampos and Ms. Janet will show you guys to your room. Do you know if your Parrain is staying with us?" He asked. I nodded my head.

"Ok. Once he finish with his phone call, he can follow you guys up to the fourth floor. We could meet back down here in two hours." He said and grabbed my hand. Kymel and Kymani grabbed their bags. They told Mr. Lampos that he didn't have to show them where their apartment was because they had been there before. They pulled out their key and jumped on the elevator with us. Tyja and Tristan didn't move from the computers. They were trying to find out everything about the men that we were up against. I knew Jo missed and was worried about Lily. He rushed up the stairs to them. Poppa walked over to Tyja and Tristan. He said something to them, which had them looking at me crazy. He nodded his head and walked off. I would have to ask Tyja about that later.

Kymani's phone interrupted the silence on the elevator. He was leaning on the wall with his head back and eyes closed. We haven't been to sleep yet. With everything going on, it was hard to close my eyes and not see the pain in my brother's. Kymani pulled out his phone and looked at the message. He smirked and was about to put his phone up, but it beeped again. He opened it up this time and the smirked became a wide grin.

"What the hell are you smiling at so hard?" I asked him. He looked over at me through his fallen dreads. Kymel was shaking his head while staring at his phone. Kymani tossed me his phone and watched my expression at a picture of a woman going down on another woman. She texted him that he was missed. Jason looked on the screen and smiled.

"I don't know why you asked him. You knew that he was going to tell you." Jason gave his unwanted opinion. I glared at Kymani. He still had that childish smirk on his face.

"Did you just get that phone, Kymani?" Kymel asked. Kymani nodded with his eyes on mine. "I guess you got to get another." Kymel said laughing. That comment had Kymani looking at him and then back at me with a different look.

"Joel, don't break my shit." He said five seconds too late. I dropped his iPhone X with the screen facing down towards the floor. We all heard the screen shatter on the elevator floor. I gave him one of my innocent smiles. "Oh, I'm sorry Mani. I accidently stop caring that your phone was in my hand and dropped it purposely." Kymel and Jason bust out laughing. Kymani couldn't do anything but pick his useless phone up and shake his head.

"You got me." He told me. The elevator doors opened. Kymani picked up his bag and began to walk out, but decided to mush my face and ran. I tried to get to him, but Kymel ran interference and blocked me in the elevator until Mani got into his apartment. I pinched Kymel on his side and moved him out my way.

"Get yo goofy ass out my way. You always helping him." I told him.

"That's because you start it, El. Do you know how long it's going to take for him to get a new phone? We can't get nothing delivered here until all this shit is over. He will have to use a burner phone."

Kymel explained. I side-eyed him, not giving a fuck. Jason walked on the side of me, watching my interactions with my brother. Kymel's apartment was two doors down from ours. We heard the kids down the hall, where Ma-Ma was staying. "Make sure she get some sleep. We have been up for forty-eight hours, strong." Kymel told Jason and went into his room.

Jason pulled out the key and opened our door. The apartment was spacious. It had a large living area with high ceilings. There was a wide portrait window that looked over the city and a full kitchen with all the appliances. All three bedrooms had their own full bath. It was beautiful.

"I am going to run your bath water. You need to soak." I told Jason and took a step forward. Jason jerked me back and stared at me. I tried to read him, but he wasn't showing me shit. After a few minutes, he finally told me what he was thinking.

"What happened with you and your brothers' mother, El?" He asked me.

I sighed and shook my head. "Not now, Jason. Let's get you in the tub and in the bed." I told him and tried to pull him towards the bedroom. He didn't budge. It felt like I was pulling a dump truck. He snatched away from me and folded his arms.

"Don't shut down on me, El. Talk to me." He said.

I looked at him and rolled my eyes. I hated when he did shit like that. If I wasn't ready to talk about the shit, why force me? I walked to the sectional that was sitting in the middle of the room. I flopped down on it and placed my hand on my knees as I recalled the day that I killed Vea.

"Poppa started my intense training after fourteen. I would practice with him throughout the summer and come back home with workout plans from my Parrain. Usually, one of my brothers would stay with my mom to make sure that she wasn't touched, while the other would come with me. She loved them for that. She would fuss at them like she was their mother." I laughed at how funny Mom would look with her finger pointed up at Kymani or Kymel's face. One time, she pulled a chair to them and climbed

on top of it to be face to face with them. They did held their laughter in until she left the room.

"One Summer, they both came with me. When it was time for me to go back home, they stayed an extra week because they wanted to have lunch with their mother. I couldn't wait for them, because school was starting up in two days. I came home from my first day as a senior in high school to my father sitting at the table talking to my mother. I thought that he was there to talk about my first day of school. But he wasn't. He told me that he had a very important job for me. I was nervous at first, because my mom didn't like us talking about shit like that around her. That time, she was angry and agreed with the mission.

Poppa got a doctor's note from one of his friends to excuse me from being absent from school. He took me to Jamaica and showed me pictures of what she looked like and where she stayed. I studied her movements for two days. Everything that Poppa had on her was accurate. I waited for nightfall to kill her. I entered the house quietly and heard someone talking. I peeped in the room and saw Vea sitting in a rocking chair. She was talking to herself. His love is an addictive drug that I no longer want to be on. She repeated that over and over, while cutting herself. It was like she was looking for another outlet.

She wanted to experience physical pain than her emotional one. I stood behind her and watched her cover her arm up with small cuts. I guess she felt me there, because she looked back at me and sneered. You will never have his heart. His heart belongs to the devil. She said to me and jumped up from her seat. I didn't know who she was talking about at that time.

She charged at me with the knife and I effortlessly removed it from her hand and stabbed her in the forehead with it. "She don't have a heart, Joel. Remove the one that she was mistakenly given to her and bring it to me," was what my father told me. I cut her heart out and placed her back in her rocking chair. I gave my father her heart and swore that I saw a tear fall from his face. I didn't understand why he would shed a tear for someone he ordered for me to kill. Keep this kill to yourself, Baby Girl. Your brothers don't have to know about this kill. He said to me and brought me back to the states.

A week later, Kymel came to my house with his arm in a sling. I asked *him what happened and he told me that they were dodging bullets. I asked about his dinner with his mother and he told me that it went well. He knew if he would have told me the truth that his mother was going to die. His mother tried to kill him more than once and he expected her to live after each time.*" I finished. Jason was standing over me. I didn't see or hear him move.

"His mother tried to kill him." He asked.

"Yeah. She tried to kill them both, Jason. What was I supposed to do?" I asked him.

"You did what was needed, El. Your brothers knew that. If they didn't forgive or understand what you did, they wouldn't be here. I was surprised that your father didn't handle her ass up when she tried to kill them the first time." Jason asked while sitting next to me.

"He was about to. They begged him to let her live. But what was crazy about that kill, was that something in my head was telling me to feel something. Remorse, sad, or angry. I felt neither. It must have been God nudging those feelings in me, because two days later, my mother died of a heart attack. My brothers and I lost our mothers in the same week." I answered.

Jason was stunned. I didn't like talking about my mother because it was the type of pain that I couldn't get rid of. "El," Jason called out. I felt my nose burning and knew that I was on the verge of tears. I shook my head and waved my hand.

"I'm good, Jason." I told him. Jason looked at me and wanted to continue with the conversation. But he knew the feeling when people brought up his father. He would try his best to ignore that subject.

Jason grabbed my hand and started rubbing on it. I looked in his wandering eyes and smiled. "I know that your mother is a sore subject that you don't want to talk about. But I am here whenever you ready." He told me. I knew it took a lot for him to say that. I kissed his lips and felt the tension in his lips. I pulled back and waited for him to talk to me. If he wanted. He smiled at me and dropped his head back, knowing that I knew that he was worried about something.

"I don't want my brothers around when we fight Matthews. I have been having this bad feeling about them being involved. That was one of the reasons why I called up Stipes and Sincere." He said.

"Are your feelings usually spot on?" I asked.

"Yeah. Always." He said and picked his head back up. "I can't lose my brothers, El." He mumbled. I knew that he was still carrying the weight of his father's death around. I put my hand on his face to get his attention.

"Talk to them Jason. Let them know how you feel." I told him. He snorted at me.

"You know that Jordan and Joseph will not back down from having my back. Jordan still feels that he have to prove something to me and he don't. You know that I am over that shit." He said. I didn't know what to tell him or how we could get them to sit this one out. I dropped my hand to his shoulder and felt how tense he was. I was going to get with Tyja after this.

"Are you ready for your bath now?" I asked him.

"Fuck no. I am ready to relive this dream I had." He said and pulled me on top, to straddle him.

"Are you sure that you are up for this? I have a whole lot of pent-up frustration." I asked while licking his lips. He smacked me on my ass and caught my bottom lip with his teeth. He pushed up and I felt how hard my special stick was.

"What you think?" He said and flipped me over.

7

MATTHEWS

I was surprised. We haven't heard anything yet about Jason burning the city down looking for us. He had to know that his family was dead. I had Roc and Badrik sitting outside guarding the house, 'til we knew for sure that they didn't know where we were. Geronimo was outside and heard a car crash into something. We thought that was Jason, but didn't see anything on our security feed. We had cameras set up within a ten mile radius of the house.

We saw when Jason's family was removed from their home and brought to the airstrip. Roc and Badrik followed them to Jamaica. He planted the bomb on the plane and came back to the states on Badrick's family private jet. His resources were working out well for us at the moment. But something about the quietness of the streets weren't sitting well with me. I picked up the phone and called Roc.

"Come back to base." I told him and hung up. Geronimo saw the frustration on my face and knew that I was one minute away from killing Luis or Badrik.

Luis was on his phone the entire time. I didn't know who he was talking to but he was getting on my fucking nerves. Looking at him was making me crazier. Roc and Badrik walked through the door. Badrik's face was of confusion.

"What's up?" He asked.

I stood and looked at him. Roc went and took a seat next to Geronimo. "You tell me." I said to him.

"I don't know what you are talking about. We placed the bomb on the plane, just like you wanted us to do." Badrik jumped on defense.

"Yeah, but it was your connect that told us that they were on the way and on that plane." I told him. "Do you have any reason to think that, that person would lie to you?" I asked him. He shook his head.

"No. We have been planning this for years. There is no way he would get this wrong." Badrik said.

He pulled out his phone and checked it. "I don't have any new messages from him. What if Jason don't know about his family being on the plane." He asked instead. Badrik didn't look sure about nothing at that point. I had to set another plan in motion. I knew that taking out the Davis' businesses weren't going to rattle Jason too much. His name wasn't on them. It was more for his brothers. I wanted them to come out and show themselves so that we could get them by themselves. They didn't take the bait either. Jason must've put them on game. I knew that I had to tag Jason's family to get the reaction that I was looking for. I needed him to act out on pure rage. He was the best at what he did and I give him that. Even when his mind was going mad, he was going to be hard to beat. But, I had a plan for that as well.

"Contact Ahmad. Send him the news feed of his brother being killed and found. He, of course, will be looking to get revenge." I told Roc. I looked over at Luis, "Are your girls still fucking with Kymani Bailey?"

"Yeah they are." He answered.

"Tell them to text him to see if he respond. That will give us the confirmation that they are still alive." I told him. He picked up his phone and called the women up. They had been fucking with him for three weeks.

"I need to go back to Jamaica and check on my mother. Callum threatened her. He had his daughter with him. She knows what her father do and what he did to her brothers' Mom. Callum is pissed now that his secret is out and will be ready to shut my mother up." Badrik said.

"Your mother will be fine. If Callum wanted your mother dead, she would have been. He wouldn't have cared that his daughter was present. What I don't understand is why a man that lethal, have children that can't fend for themselves." I thought out loud.

"Yeah. That is some crazy shit." Roc said. "I have seen pictures of Joel. A woman that beautiful with a father that powerful, should be guarded at all times." You could see the frown on Badrik's face when Roc made the comment. His stupid ass was in love with the woman. I didn't expect him to go with us blowing the plane up with the woman on the plane. He looked relieved that there was a possibility with them being alive. Luis did too. I felt a headache coming.

"Don't worry about it. I will send some people to take care of Callum. You take care of your unreliable connects, before he get you killed." I said to him. I pulled out my phone and made a call.

"Levy. I thought you forgot about us. We had been waiting for our time to make an entrance." Eliria's voice came through my phone.

"Callum. He would be the first." I told her.

"Good. I always wanted to go to Jamaica." She giggled.

JORDAN

I WAS happy to have my family back. After hearing what went down in Jamaica, I was sure that they would be safer here with me. As bad as I wanted Lily, I needed to be around my boys right now. We were all cuddled up in the King size bed watching Wreck'it Ralph 2. I didn't understand shit that was going on with the movie. JoJo was happy and that's all that matters. Jerimiah was laying on my bare chest sleeping. JoJo was a splitting image of me, but Jerimiah looked just like Jason. I guess it was true what they say about the baby will come out looking like the one that got on your nerves or almost drove you to insanity. At that time, Jason was doing a lot of that with everyone.

Lily walked out the bathroom with her robe on. Her hair was wet and up in a towel. She carried that baby weight well. She looked over at me and smiled. "Don't even think about." She told me.

"What?" I played innocent.

"I haven't been able to see my doctor yet about any birth control. I am not having any more children 'til Jerimiah gets older." She complained. To who? I didn't know. Because that birth control shit was for couples that were dating or just fucking. We were married. If she got pregnant again, oh well. I knew that I was talking that shit about Jerimiah being the last one. I said the same thing about JoJo.

It was something about how I was feeling when Lily was pregnant with my children. It was indescribable. I knew after this was all over, Jason was going to try and knock up Joel. And the way JJ and Tyja was going at it since she came back, she was going to pop up pregnant soon. Ma was going to have a house full of grandchildren.

"Eff birth control." I said to her while staring at Jerimiah. I heard her ass make some type of noise and walked out the bedroom. Her and that smart ass mouth was going to get her fucked up. You know what. Fuck that. She was about to get fucked up. I lifted baby boy up and placed him on the bed next to JoJo.

"Stay in here and watch your movie. I am going to help Mommy with some snacks for you."

"That's cool, Dad. Can I have some of the gummy bears, too?" He asked.

"Yea, Lil Man." I told him and walked out the room. I heard her moving around in the kitchen. I knew that our time for intimacy was always clutched. We had to get it in, where we fit in. Ma helped a lot, but Lily was the kind of woman that she needed to be around the children all the time. I mean all the time. And there was nothing wrong with that. But when it was time to find someone to watch them, the baby would cry. She did the exact same thing with JoJo. The only people that JoJo wanted to be under was his Mom. He cried every time she left the room. I told her that we wasn't going to do that this time around. Jerimiah's ass was goin on sleepovers at one.

I walked in the kitchen and watched her prepare bottles for Jerimiah so that she didn't have to do all that in the middle of the night. Her ass looked like a round peach in her robe. I wanted to bite it to see how juicy it was. It had to be. I went over to her and bent to take a nice bite on her right ass cheek. She giggled and moaned at the same time.

"I already told you what it was." She said not sounding too sure.

"I heard you talking, but that shit don't have nothing to do with me." I told her and bit the other cheek. She made her ass jump and that bitch jiggled. *Fuck.*

I raised her robe up and looked down at my favorite fruit. I smacked it and watched a tidal wave appear. Lily moaned again and bent over. Her ass wasn't slick. She was talking all that noise about not doing nothing and her freaky ass was already throwing caution out of the window. I didn't argue with her. I pulled my basketball shorts down with my boxers and teased her opening with her dick. She pushed back on it, hating the teasing part.

"Look at yo hungry ass. That pussy hungry, huh." I teased her some more. She glared at me over her shoulder where my name was tatted.

"You know how your son is." She said. I didn't need her to say anything else. I eased my way into my special place that was gonna have me forgetting about my reality. "Oh shit Jo." She groaned out.

By the way her walls squeezed and pulled on my dick, I should have been the one moaning. I didn't know how she was doing it, but I loved it. I grabbed her ass and slid in and out that pussy. Lily looked back at me and grabbed my shirt. She threw one of her legs on the counter. I bent my knees to get deeper in that pussy. "Fuck!" I yelled. I couldn't hold that one in. My baby was twerking on my shit like a porn star. Our bodies were making smacking noises that almost drowned out the sound to the movie in our bedroom. I pulled my shirt up and tucked it underneath my chin. I pulled out and pushed back in slowly. She was chasing after her nut, but I was prolonging that muthafucker.

"Naw, you gon' bust when I tell you to." I told her. I peeled that robe off her body and snatched that towel from her head. Her damp hair fell in her face. I grabbed and wrapped her hair around my hand to pull her up. She kept the arch in her back and turned to me. I kissed her sweet lips and began stroking her again. She pulled away from my mouth and started chanting.

"Shit. Shit. Shit."

I placed my other hand on her hip and pulled her back to meet my strokes. "You about to have another one. You know that right." I told her feeling myself getting close.

"No, Jo-Jordan. Wa-Wait ah min-," she tried to say. Once again, I was deaf as fuck. I wasn't hearing shit that she had to say. I let her hair go and grabbed her waist with both hands.

"Jordan, please." She begged. I went harder with every stroke that led me to an earthshattering orgasm. I wasn't only deaf, but blind as well. I was seeing white and black spots. I threw my hand up on the cabinet to catch me from falling on Lily. We both were breathing hard. Our combined juices were running down her leg. She was going to be mad for real. But, I was ready to deal with it.

I pushed off the cabinet and pulled out of her gently. I walked to the laundry room and grabbed one of the towels there. I walked back to the kitchen sink, wet it, and walked back to Lily. She was standing straight up with her back turned towards me. I kneeled before her and turned her to face me. The scowl on her face had me joked out. Lily was a beautiful woman. When she tried to look angry it looked too cute to take seriously.

"I told you that I wasn't trying to get pregnant again." She scolded me. I picked up her leg and began cleaning her up. She couldn't hold the scowl on her face when I began to clean those tempting lips. She threw her head back and moaned again. Freak.

"I know what you said Lily. But you have to understand that I ain't no random nigga. I am your husband. I don't want to hear shit about birth control or anything else that will prevent you from getting pregnant." I told her and kissed her thigh.

"Jordan, my body needs rest. I just had a baby. Why can't we wait like we did with Jerimiah?" She asked.

"Because I want to get them all out of the way now." I told her. Lily's eyes got wide and she took her leg out my hand.

"What do you mean by all?" She asked but couldn't finish. JoJo's voice came through the door.

"Mommy, I think Jerimiah is hungry. He is in here sucking on my face." He said with laughter. I threw the towel in the dirty laundry basket and grabbed one of the bottles off the counter.

"I got it. Go and take another shower." I told her and kissed her softly on the lips. She shook her head and smiled.

"You know that this isn't over." I ignored her and went to feed my son.

"Daddy where is the snacks?" He asked. *Shit.*

"Your mother is bringing them in." I told him and, on my word, Lily came in there with the gummy bears and a bottle of water. She walked back into the bathroom and ran the shower. JoJo looked over at me and stared.

"What's wrong JoJo?" I asked him while feeding a wide awake Jerimiah.

"How come every time you are with Mommy alone you get her dirty? She never looks it, but she always have to take a shower when you two get alone." He asked. Dude was always asking questions and shit.

"She waste juice on herself this time. She wiped it off but it made her sticky." I told him.

"Oh, she is clumsy like Aunt Joel. Uncle Jason told Mason the same thing." He said and turned to watch the movie. I shook my head and laughed.

Once the family was sound asleep, I went back downstairs to check on things. I had to call all my business partners to inform them of the threat. A lot of them agreed and a few of them wanted to pull out of our business agreement. I knew that they were scared for their family's lives and for their own. I talked to my lawyer and told them to prepare the necessary paperwork for that to be done. I wasn't going to keep them in a business that was threatening their livelihood.

I got to the first floor where everyone was gathered. Joel's Parrain and Callum was sitting at one of the tables having a drink. Jason looked like he done had his daily dose of Joel, which was a good thing. When I saw the plane blow up on the screen, my heart dropped. I didn't feel anything at that moment. Jason stormed out and didn't hear shit that no one said. I was about to follow him but my phone began to beep. I pulled it out and got a text from Lily, saying that they was alright. Tyja screamed out to Jason but he was already in the car. Sincere ran after him. Stipes told us that it would have been better if Sincere went, since they didn't know that they were in town.

"Aye, no word yet." I asked them. JJ shook his head.

"Nah. That bitch didn't call yet." He responded. I walked over to the group and listened in.

"Alright, he said that he was pissed that you killed his sister." Sincere said.

"He didn't kill his sister, Madison did." Kymel said. They didn't believe in giving other people credit for their work. Madison and Mason wasn't any different. Stipes and Sincere looked over at Joel and Jason.

"Are you fucking serious?" Stipes asked. Jason smiled and nodded his head.

"How did she do it?" Sincere asked like a kid asking for a bedtime story.

"She did it with an injector knife." Joel answered. Stipe made a T with his hands.

"Timeout. Can you please tell me how that was possible?" He asked. I looked from Joel and Jason, to see if they were going to tell them who Joel and her brothers really were. Callum and the Punisher stopped their conversation. The whole room got quiet. Joel nodded her head and Jason looked back at his Seal brothers. "Do you know the hand and hand combat that we learned in the beginning of our Seal training?" He led off with.

"Yeah," Stipes answered. Jason pointed behind him towards the Punisher.

"He was the one to create the training module. That is the Punisher." Jason told them. They looked back at the Punisher and was just as shocked as we were.

"No bullshit?" Sincere asked.

"No bullshit." The Punisher answered.

"It's a fucking honor, Man." Stipes saluted him. Punisher held up his drink.

"You remember when I used to talk about the assassins that my father hired when I wasn't around. That is the Callum that I talked about. Kymani, Kymel, and Joel are the Elites." He told them. He pointed to Kymel and introduced him as Shadow and Kymani as Reaper. He then pointed to Joel and introduced her as Gage. Sincere's eyes went straight to Joel. You could see the disbelief in his eyes. The last time someone told Joel that she wasn't Gage, she showed them by yanking the throat out of a big muthafucker.

"I could see that you two have some killer instincts to y'all. But, come on Joel. You sung on my stage. I don't see it in you." He told her. Stipes was still silent with the information about the Punisher.

"She alright." Kymel told him. "But, we trained my niece and nephew to protect themselves, if need be." He said.

"Ok," Stipes shook his head and continued. "My sweet little niece killed Sierra. Matthews caught wind of that and decided to move on with his plan quicker than he wanted." Stipes said.

"Wait. Sierra's death wasn't too long ago." I said. "Matthews been planning to take Jason out?" I asked.

"Yes. When he found out that Jason had children, he put his plan into motion. He always thought that kids of our blood, killer's blood, shouldn't exist." Sincere said.

"I left home, baby. To be with my side piece. My side piece." We heard a ringtone went off. Joel glared at her father.

"I told you to change that Poppa. You got Mason singing that song." She told him. Callum hunched his shoulders and pulled out his phone.

"Winston," he answered.

"Then you got it as a ringtone to every call. You have to give that ringtone to your sidepieces only, Pops." Kymani said and shook his head. "You don't want people thinking you playing for the other team."

Callum ignored him and listened to the other end. "What's up Winston?"

"Oh, I'm sorry Callum. Winston is not doing too well. He is trying to breathe, but the hole in his chest is making that impossible." We heard the woman say. Callum stood up and walked over to us with Punisher following behind him.

"Who the fuck is this?" Callum's voice boomed out.

"Come on Callum. Has it been that long? Well maybe it has. The last time I talked to you, you were on your way to France to kill my father for my bitch of a mother. So, I guess it has been a while." The woman said. Callum's face changed dark and was ready to jump through the phone.

"Eliria, what the fuck are you doing at my house?" Callum asked.

"I was looking for you, of course. I thought that we could have sat down and had a chat. You and I have so much to discuss." Eliria told him.

"What do you want to talk about, Eliria? Because you being at my house, unannounced is telling me that a chat was not going to happen." Callum said to her. Joel and her brothers were seething. Joel's eyes were slits.

"That is true, Callum. It was going to be that or you could have brought out your Elites. We have been wanting to meet them for years. Why do you keep them in the dark, Callum?" She said with her French accent seeping through.

"I don't think that I need the Elites for you and your pussy ass brothers." He replied.

"Wow, Callum. I didn't know that your old bones could do those things still." She said smiling. "Can you be a doll and just tell us where you are? This cat and mouse shit that Matthews has us doing is really boring. I hoped that we can meet up and just get this over with. I do have a couple of things that I want to talk about. Maybe you need a reason to seek me." She said. The phone went quiet and gun shots rang through. "Because killing your men, won't do shit to get you here. Your kids must be ok, if you haven't killed Abigail yet. Hmm." She said thinking. "Maybe if I could speak to your daughter, Joel. Maybe she could get you to come meet me with your Elites." She told him.

Callum looked over to Joel. He didn't know if she was ready to play that game with Eliria. Joel reached for the phone. Callum gave it to her hesitantly.

"Hello," Joel spoke with control.

"Hi Sweetheart. How are you?" Eliria asked.

"I am doing well and yourself." She asked.

"Great. Is this a private conversation?" She asked.

"No. Do you need it to be?" Joel asked her.

"No. I wish that we could have this conversation face to face. I really would like to put a face to this sweet voice." She said.

"Well, Eliria, is it?" Joel asked while sitting in front of the computer.

"Yes it is my dear." Eliria responded.

"You are in luck. I am in front of my computer. If you want we can do face time." Joel asked.

"No, my sweetheart. Face time doesn't capture the feelings and the emotion that I want to experience when we have our little talk. Maybe we could meet up for some tea. I will promise you that I or anyone else won't harm you. If you are afraid, you can always asked for some guards to come with you or the man that you are with. I am pretty sure that he would defend you with his life." Eliria said. Joel sat and thought about what she said. You could see that she was ready to meet the woman that threatened her father.

"How do I know that you would keep your word? You could be trying to kidnap me and turn me over to Matthews." Joel asked.

"I give you my word, sweetheart. Matthews is after your

boyfriend, not you. Badrik wanted you at first but the way you talked to his mother has him rethinking things. You could ask your father. When a Cassel give our word, we stand by it." She said. We all looked over at Callum and he nodded his head.

"Okay, we can do that. When and where?" Joel answered. You could hear clapping over the phone.

"Fabulous. I will text your father's phone with a time for tomorrow. You guys are in Philly correct." She asked. I didn't think that Joel would give her that information, but she did.

"Good. See ya soon." She said and hung up. Joel passed the phone back to her father.

"What will be the purpose of this meeting?" Jason asked. He was pissed that she didn't asked no one if the shit was okay to do or not.

"Like her, I am tired of this cat and mouse shit. I say we meet up, everybody pick a man or woman to fight and get this shit over with." Joel said and stormed off. Jason didn't follow behind her. Tyja jumped up and went after her sister. I agreed with Joel. I was ready for this shit to be over with. I felt like I was hiding from an ass whipping.

JJ walked up, rubbing his hands together. "Shit. I wish I was there when Joel reveal to them who she really is."

"Why," Tank asked.

"It's like Steven Segal in *Under Siege*, when people find out how lethal Casey Ryback is. They start pulling out the big guns but it be too late. Casey Ryback had already fucked everybody up." He said. Sincere nodded his head and agreed with his stupid ass.

"For real, Bruh. You ain't never lying." He said. Everybody else shook their heads.

"Let me talk to you three for a minute." Jason pointed at me, Tank, and JJ. We walked out of the door and went into the office. Jason went and sat behind his desk. We sat and waited for him to talk.

"Aight. I have been thinking about this a lot now and I think that it would be best if you guys would sit this one out." He said. I frowned my face up and sat back in my seat. I knew this fool wasn't talking about going to war with these crazy ass niggas without us.

"What the fuck are you talking about?" I spat out. Jason closed his eyes and took a deep breath.

"Look, I don't want to lose any of you. I don't think that I could live with that type of loss. I can't deal with any of your deaths on my head, Man." He mumbled.

"Fuck that, Nigga! Are you serious right now? I ain't leaving you out there by your fucking self J. You are my fucking brother. I can't believe you asking us to do this." JJ jumped up and said. Tank looked like he was about to flip the desk over on his ass.

"Y'all not making this shit easy." He said. It was my turn to stand up. I took the chair that I was sitting in and threw that bitch to the wall. I speared his ass with a look.

"I don't give a fuck what you feeling or what you were thinking. We are going to be by your side 'til this shit is resolved. We should be the ones that have your back out there. Us. If something was to happen to you that is another death that I would have to live with. You ain't gon' do this shit." I told his ass, dead serious. He sat back and was about to say something but I wasn't trying to hear that shit. I walked out the door and slammed that bitch, putting a crack in the door. We just got our relationship right. It was my turn to be the big brother and protect him at all cost.

8

JASON

I watched my big brother stand his ground and walk out my office. I haven't seen Jo that pissed in a while and he should be. It was something about this fight that had me feeling some type of way. The last time that happened, I let my father walk out the door. I wasn't about to do a repeat with my brothers.

"I don't know what the fuck got you thinking that way, Bruh. And before you fix your mouth to explain yourself, I'm going to tell you this." JJ told me. He walked over to the desk, placed both hands on it, and leaned forward. "You worried about how you would feel. Just imagine how we would feel, if we could have prevented your death and didn't do shit about it. That would drive us crazy, Bruh." He told me and stood up straight. JJ always had us laughing and joked out. But this JJ, was someone that you wouldn't want to see in the streets. He wanted me to object to anything he said, so that he could box me up. "That's what I thought." JJ said and took the same exit.

Tank was the only one left staring at me like I lost my fucking mind. "What are you feeling, J?" Tank asked me.

"I got this bad feeling, Tank. In my heart, I know that something bad is going to happen. I just don't know what it is. I don't want you guys to get hurt or killed behind my shit, T. I wouldn't be able to explain that shit to my Ma, T Glen, or Lily. Fuck! How am I going to explain that to JoJo or Jerimiah when they get older? I can't let y'all be out there with me like that. Not this go round." I explained to him. Tank sighed and dropped his elbows on his knees. He knew what I was talking about. He witnessed what happened when I got those feelings.

"I hear you, J. But there is no way that Jo or JJ is going to back down from this. You are their little brother, Man. They are not going to let you swim in that water by yo self." He said and stood up to leave.

"Aye, who is the chick that you got pregnant?" I asked him. He stopped at the door and dropped his head down.

"How did you know?" He mumbled.

"Tristan ass gave you away. He kept looking at you while T Glen was grilling him. You know he can't keep a secret." I said. He turned back around and smiled.

"And," he dug. I stood and walked over to him.

"You were thinking about the chances of you not meeting your child. Or her not meeting the family. You want to be there for your baby. When you are a father in this business, you do a lot of second guessing." I told him.

"Yeah. I have been doing that a lot lately. I wanted to bring her here but I didn't want to put that target on her back if people don't know about her." Tank replied.

"When are we going to meet her?" I asked him.

"After this shit is over. We planned on doing a gender reveal party." He said with a smile. I dapped him off and congratulated him. T Glen was going to spoil the fuck outta that kid. She already was doing it to ours. I walked out of the office and back into the lobby with Tank. Jo and JJ were giving me the evil eyes as I walked in. I had to try. Sin looked up at me. "Feeling." He asked.

"Yeah. I don't think that my brothers should be there with us. I know that something will happen to them if they go. I know that their stubborn asses is going to make their way to wherever we go." I told him.

"I can put them in a sleeper or shoot them somewhere." Stipes said. I looked up at him to see if his ass was serious or not. He looked at me with his eyebrows bunched up.

"Nigga what?" I asked him.

"Pick one. They will be alright." He said.

"Shut the fuck up Stipes." I told him and went upstairs to check on Joel. She was outside her damn mind to think that she was going to meet with them crazy muthafuckers. We didn't know what kind of conversation that Eliria wanted to have with Joel. I hope that it wasn't nothing drastic to have her skinning her alive in public. I got to our room and heard Tyja trying to talk sense in her.

"Joel, this is not a good idea. What if she is lying? What if they do try and take you?" Tyja asked. I didn't wait for her to answer. I walked in and waited for her answer. Joel looked at me and rolled her eyes.

"I already said why. I am tired of this shit. I am ready to move on and live. If they want to be labeled as the greatest assassin, they are going to do this fair and easy. They don't want help from Matthews to accomplish this." Joel said. She looked up at Tyja. "Can you please go get the kids?" She asked. Tyja looked over at me before leaving. She wanted me to try and talk Joel out of her decision.

"Don't start with your shit, Jason." She said to me without looking up.

"What shit? Because your safety will not be described as shit." I told her. She glared up at me this time.

"You do understand that I am the deadliest person here." She told me.

"You are also a mother, a sister, a daughter, and a fucking wife. But you seem to forget that when you decide that it is okay to put yourself in unnecessary danger." I told her.

"Whatever, Jason. My children and family are the reason why I agreed to do this." She said and tried to walk off. I grabbed her by the waist and pulled her in front of me. She didn't struggle, like I thought she would. She fell into my arms and sighed. She was worried but didn't want to show it. "You don't have to be tough all the time, Joel. We do have people here that can help. I am one of them." I told her.

"I know," she whispered. The door opened and in walked the twins. Madison ran over to us, while Mason lingered behind with headphones on.

"What are you listening to?" I asked him and pulled off his headphones.

"J. Cole new album *KOD*. Uncle Mel and Uncle JJ was listening to some days ago. It's pretty good." He answered. I placed the headphones on my ears. It had a nice beat to it. I passed his headphone back to him. "What's up, Dad?" Joel picked Madison up and walked to the couch and sat.

"Daddy and I will be going out soon. We will need you guys to be on your best behavior. Kymel and Kymani are coming with us." She told them. Madison grabbed her mother's face and turned it towards her.

"You coming back, right." She asked.

"Yes, we are. I just need you to understand that the situation is dangerous and there are people out to kill us, again. But these people are professionals. If they approach any of you, you take them out quickly because there would be more coming. Protect and watch each other's back. Do you understand?" I told them.

"Yes, Dad," Mason answered. Madison nodded her head and leaned against her mother. "Can we play a game?" Mason asked.

"Of course. What do you want to play?" Joel asked. Mason ran out the room and came back with a board game. Madison picked her head up and yelled that she was yellow. Mason placed the game of Trouble on the table.

"I haven't played this in a minute." I said and sat next to Joel.

"Be careful, Daddy, Mason cheats." Madison said while setting up her yellow pieces. I looked at Mason and he had a smirk on his face.

"They always think that I cheat, because I win all the time. Tell them that that is called greatness, Dad." He said setting up his green pieces. Joel shook her head at him. Mason was always talking shit. He hated losing. When we played 2K his ass would miraculously start the game all over. He got that shit from JJ. It was comical watching them two play. We played with the kids and had our family time 'til

Eliria texted Callum with the address and time. I told Sin and Stipes to take over the security at the apartment. Jordan and Joseph was going to keep an eye on things on the inside. Tristan and Tank was going to keep a close eye on the house that Matthews was in. Callum and Punisher was staying behind for more protection. I didn't understand how he was comfortable with letting Joel go to this meeting. I was on the edge about it and was ready to call this shit off.

We were already on the way to the restaurant that sat in the middle of the busy city. Kymel and Kymani was in the front seat while we were in the back. Joel was wearing what she called a strapless romper. I didn't know what it was called but it had her body looking delicious. The color was burnt orange. It matched her complexion and her blonde curly hair.

"I am going to stay in the car, Joel. If I see anything that looks like a trap, we coming through shooting the place up." Kymani told her. She nodded her head while looking out of the window. If she was nervous, she didn't show it. Baby girl looked relaxed and ready.

We pulled up at the corner of the place. Mani reached back and gave her kiss on the nose. She smiled at him and waited for me to come around and open the door. She took my hand and placed a sweet kiss on my lips. "Don't give in to shit they say, ok." She told me. I kissed her again, longer this time. The first time in life, I was going to step back and let her take lead. We walked in the restaurant hand in hand to the guest check station with Kymel.

"Reservations for Bailey and Cassel." Joel asked. The guy looked at her and smiled. "Right this way Ma'am." The waiter answered and led us to a private section in the restaurant. The restaurant was large and the place was packed. We bumped into a couple of people before getting to the table with Eliria and her brothers. Eliria's brothers stood up and sized us up. Kymel looked like an average Joe. He had on khaki pants and a red polo shirt. His dreads piled up neatly in one of his hair ties. He stood on Joel's left and I was on her right.

Eliria stood up and greeted us. "Welcome. You must be Joel." She said and reached out her hand. Joel shook her hand.

"Yes, this is Jason and my brother Kymel." She introduced. Her eyes wandered on us and then back to Joel. "It must be nice to be surrounded by such beautiful men. Please have a sit." She asked. Kymel checked the chairs before we took the seat. There were food and drinks already on the table. I didn't trust nothing on this table. I pushed the plate aside and leaned back from the table.

"I am here. Talk." Joel said. Eliria looked at her and laughed.

"I love it. A woman that don't procrastinate and get straight to the point. I think that men are the great procrastinators. They say us women don't know what we want, but we tell them straight. This is what we want and how we want it. They get distracted and go another route and get us the generic brand. And then they get pissed off when we stab them in the neck." She said. I didn't understand nothing this bitch just said. I kept my eyes on her brother that was sitting in front of me. His eyes lingered on Joel a minute too long for my liking. I had to remind myself that this was Joel's show.

Eliria looked at her brothers and introduced them. "This is Antione, my oldest brother. He is known to have fist like hammers, like his assassin name. Enzo is the second oldest. His assassin name is Raine; came from his work. Whenever he is done with a hit, the amount of blood spatters looks like blood have drizzled its way in. And of course your father has warned you about me. The Storm. The oh, so sweet, quiet Storm. No matter how much you prepare for it. It will always hit. And it will always destroy." She said and picked up her cup. She took a sip and stared at Joel over her cup.

Joel maintained eye contact, showing no expressions about what Eliria said. She looked like she was ready to go. "The talk, Eliria. You do understand that I have better things to do." Joel spoke.

"Yes. The talk. But first, can I ask you a question? Have you talked to your father's Elite team? I am pretty sure that after finding out what Gage has done to your brother's mother was shocking, but well deserved." She said looking over to Kymel. "Vea was cursed of motherhood. Something that she didn't deserve to be. On the other hand, Ms. Cassidy was a prized mother." She said and looked back at Joel. Joel expressions were still blank but her eyes was telling a story by itself. She was ready to kill Eliria already.

"Ms. Cassidy. She was sweet and kind. You were her priority. She didn't go around chasing Callum's confused ass. She placed all her focus on you. I was jealous of that. That special bond you had with your mother couldn't be replaced by anyone else. I can understand why you wouldn't want to talk about her. It hurts. Unlike my mother, who tried to kill the only person that really loved us. She was selfish. I didn't regret killing her. If I could have done it again I would." She said with a quick smile. It dropped and was replaced with sadness and remorse. "But…I do regret killing yours." She said while looking at Joel.

Heat from Joel's body could have warmed the coldest room. Joel bald her fist up and closed her eyes. Kymel's eyes were on Eliria's face. I didn't know how to react to this fucking news. I was ready for whatever my baby wanted to do. If we had to tear down this whole restaurant with everybody in it, I was down. The pain and hurt that I knew she was feeling was going to boil over quick.

"You see. The emotions and your feelings has changed the atmosphere in this room. I wouldn't have been able to feel this over facetime. Your anger. Is…Wow! It feels familiar." She said. Antione and Enzo were watching Joel. Joel's eyes opened and she was no longer that sweet young woman that walked in. She was now the person that shook the souls of men. Eliria's brothers felt it. You could hear the pitch in their breath. Eliria shifted in her seat uncomfortably.

"My mother died of a heart attack." Joel whispered deadly. Eliria tapped her finger on the table and let out a sigh.

"Your mother was a very healthy woman, Joel. Your family history doesn't have relatives with heart issues either. It was the tea that she and I had. I was in town and your father came to pick you up to go and see your brother Kymel when he was in the hospital. Antoine and I talked to her about an exchange program in France that you were interested in. She told us that you went to visit your father and was due to come home that day. I was supposed to give her the strongest dose of the poison, so that she could die quick. You was supposed to come home to her cold body. But the way that she talked about you, made me change my mind. I wanted you to have more days with her. When I heard she died, I wept. I cried as if she was my own mother." She said and picked up her napkin to catch the falling tears from her eyes. "But. A job is a job." Eliria finished. Joel took in a deep breath and exhaled. She pulled her bloody hands from underneath the table and placed them on the table. Her fists were bald so tight, that her nails cut into her skin.

"Di death dat yuh had given mi mada wud be di death dat yuh beg fi. Yuh did hoping dat dis information wi lead yuh to di Elites. It ave. But, it also lead yuh to a dawta whose mada did taken from har. A dawta dat had taking lives fi har. Di dawta dat kill wid no remorse. No regrets. Wen mi dun wid yuh Eliria yuh wi be cryin fi death an mi doubt dat mi sick an twist mind wi gi inna." Gage spoke with a sinister smile. Eliria sat back with confusion on her face. Kymel leaned forward.

"Yuh neva understand, let mi translate dat fi yuh." He said and repeated everything that Gage said in French. He was so pissed that he knew his English was going to be broken. Eliria's eyes widened and her brothers sat up straighter. They looked at Joel and Kymel in a different light. They stood up on the other side of the table and stood back. They were waiting for an attack. Joel opened her hand and place them flat on the table. She stood and turned to walk out. Kymel and I stood behind her just in case they wanted to attack.

"Qui êtes-vous, Joel?" Eliria asked Gage, before she got to the door. Joel turned around to face Eliria full on.

"Je suis Gage, Eliria. Mes frères sont Fictifs et Reap. Et dans quelques jours, vous avez tous sera mort avec votre père inutile." Joel told her. "Je vais certainement vous voir à nouveau." She turned with that and walked out the room. Eliria looked like she bit off more than she could chew. Antione and Enzo winked at us and promised us a good fight. We walked out the restaurant to Kymani standing outside the car. Joel reached up and yanked the hair tie out of her head. Kymani walked forward and was about to walk back into the restaurant. Kymel placed his hand on his brother's chest and pushed him back slightly.

"Wi ave fi get har outta here, now."

Kymani looked at him and then back at Gage. She was sitting in the car, calmly. Too fucking calm. I walked around and got in on the other side. I didn't say anything, because I didn't know what to tell her. Kymani jumped in the car and slammed the door. He rotated his neck and grabbed his steering wheel. Kymel jumped in the car with his dreads loose and hung in his face.

"Yuh ave a place inna mind sista." Kymani asked her, while pulling off.

"Mi duh." She answered. She was staring out of the window. I reached for her hand and looked down at the wounds that were there. She looked at me like I was foreign. She didn't want to be touched or bothered at the moment. But, I wasn't going to let her go through this shit alone. She recently confessed that when she killed Vea, something was nudging at her to feel something about what she was doing. It wasn't regret towards killing Vea, but not being there for her mom. It was guilt. She was going to think that her mother's death was her fault and that is something that no one should live with. I did and it tore me up inside. I didn't need her to think like that.

Gage tried to pull her hand away from me. I held it tightly and ripped the bottom of my shirt to wrap it. Her cuts were deep and leaking blood. After I finished wrapping it, I pulled it up to my lips and kissed it while staring into her troublesome eyes. I was letting her know that I was ready to travel down that road with her. I was going to carry all of the baggage to ensure her sanity. My face time ring went off. I pulled out and hit accept. Madison's angry face popped up.

"What's wrong, Maddie?" I asked her. I pulled the phone back from my face. Gage scooted over to see Madison's face.

"There men here. Uncle Sin and Stipes tried to keep them out the gate but one of the guys shot a missile at the gate. A few of them got into the apartment building but they were taking care of. Uncle Jo sent me up here with Mason to protect the women and the children. One of the men shot Nanny in the leg. She is fine but the men are still coming through." She explained. Kymani stepped on the gas.

"Stay upstairs 'til we get there. We are on our way." I told her. Madison nodded and looked at her mother. She frowned.

"Yuh okay mada." She asked. Mason heard Madison's voice change and grabbed the phone. Gage looked at the phone and shook her head.

"No mi nuh."

Mason looked at his mother with a scowl on his face. "Den dem wi dead." He told her. Gage nodded and hung up the phone. Gage let down the armrest that was in the middle of the backseat. That was the easy way to get to the trunk. She reached through the hole and pulled out a big bag. She placed it on my leg and opened it up. She had clothes, guns, and knives in it. She passed me the guns and started changing into her war clothes. I called JJ and Jo, but they didn't answer. I dialed Sin's number.

"Davis, where are you?" Sin answered.

"We are on our way back. What the fuck is going on?" I asked him. I heard guns going off in the background. JJ and Jo voice was heard as well. I was happy that they were around each other. I still needed to find out how Ma got shot.

"Badrik and Luis men are here. Muthafuckers blew the gate up, J. Stipes and Punisher is covering the other exit." He told me.

"Aight. We will come through the lobby office. That office is connected to the main office. Do you have eyes on Badrik or Luis?" I asked him.

"No, not yet. We will clear the way for you guys. Hurry up, though. We are running out of ammo and I am sure that they might have more men on the way." He said and hung up. As we got closer, smoke was seen in the sky near the apartment building. Everybody was locked and loaded. Kymani turned down the street and ran into six SUVS blocking the entrance of the gate. Reap parked and jumped out with the rest of us. We didn't have a plan or need one. We all had the same goal. Kill as many as possible. I pulled my two forty-five's from my holsters. Gage held her pink and gold Dessert Eagle.

Shadow walked in the gate and grabbed one of the men that was shooting at the front entrance of the building. He pulled his head back and shot him in the face. He dropped his body and began shooting at the other men around him. Gage let off a few shots, but you could see that she wanted to get her hands on somebody. She got her wish, when a man got behind her and wrapped his arms around her body. He thought that he was about to negotiate something to get his way in.

Gage grabbed the man's arm and slit his wrist with one of her knives. The man dropped his gun but didn't live long after that. She gut punched him in the stomach, which had him bending over. Gage raised her knife up and stabbed him on top of his head. She pulled the knife out and threw it at a man running towards her.

I walked towards my office door shooting muthafuckers myself. I shot my last bullet into a man that was standing in front of my office door. His friend raised up a shotgun to shoot at me. I rushed him and dodged his swing when I got closer. I pulled out my knife from my ankle holder and stabbed him in his leg. The bitch yelled and tried to hit me again. I released the empty magazine and inserted another. I hit him in the throat and placed my gun in it after it flew open from the hit. Without hesitating, I pulled the trigger and blew his brains out. I looked back and saw that the Elites were the only ones standing. I nodded my head and walked into my office. I put in my code and waited for the door to open. Once it did, we had access to more weapons. Reap and Shadow grabbed weapons for the guys. Gage walked through the door and into the lobby of the apartment building. Bullets were flying through the windows.

"Weh a mi fada." Gage asked JJ. He looked back and pointed upstairs. "He left with Tristan and Tyja. They found some shit out and left. They haven't come back yet. " JJ told her. She looked back at me and nodded. I knew baby girl was going to be alright. I blew her a kiss and watched her take the stairs. "How many more are out there?" Tank yelled. Reap reloaded his gun. "Nine." He answered and passed it to me.

I let off six shots through the wall. "Three now." I said. We heard three other shots and knew that it came from upstairs. Shadow opened the door and didn't take cover. He was that sure that they was no one else out there. He looked back and closed the door that was barely hanging on.

"None, now?" He said and went to the back of the building. Jo and JJ walked up to me.

"Those niggas were waiting for y'all to leave to come through here." Jo said. I looked them over to make sure that they were okay. When I saw that they were good I asked about Ma. "What happened to Ma?"

"Ma and T Glen was outside on the playground with the children and Lily. We were outside watching them. Mason was eyeing one of the guards. He came to me and JJ, and told us that the guards didn't work for you. We played it cool and tried to get them inside. You know your son can't hide his expressions, no he was mugging the man. Oh boy got spooked and pulled his gun out. Madison pulled out a knife and threw it in his arm, which made the gun fall from his hand. When it hit the ground it went off and hit Ma in the leg. Mason picked the gun up and empty the clip in his face. After that, all hell broke loose. Missiles and shit started flying. Niggas started pouring in like we was giving out free shit." Jo said. He nodded Sincere's way. "That Nigga right there is cold with it." He complimented.

"He should be. I taught him everything he know." I said. JJ was on the phone with Tyja.

"We good, Girl. No. Don't come back here. I will text you with another location." He told her and hung up the phone. Stipes and Punisher came walking up. "Why would he attack like that and not be sure to get what he want?" JJ asked.

"This didn't have anything to do with Matthews. This was all Badrik and Luis. They are trying to get the children and Joel before Matthews can get to them." Stipes said.

"Yeah, they have better move quick. Because I am pretty sure that Eliria is going to tell Matthews that Callum's children are the Elites." I said.

"If that's the case, we gotta move the women and children to another location. If he get that message he will come here and blow everybody up in this bitch." Sincere said. I went upstairs to check on

Ma and the children. Mason was standing by the door with his revolver. He stood up and dapped me off.

"We already packed and ready to go." He told me. I loved that he knew the game. Everyone's bag was sitting at the door. T Glen walked out of the room shaking her head.

"You see that bossy ass lil boy of yours is going to get slapped. He talking to us like he our man and shit." She complained.

"I am not acting like your man Teedy. I am acting like I love you and want to get you to safety." He said and picked up her bags. "Can you go downstairs please?" He asked. I was surprised when she walked up to him and kissed him on the top of his head.

"That Goddamn boy." She mumbled and walked down the stairs with JoJo. Ma was sitting on the couch with her leg propped up.

"How you feeling Ma?" I asked her.

"I feel like I got shot. Other than that, I am fine." She said. "Where are we going now?" She said.

I had a few more buildings in mind, but I didn't want my family in the same spot as us. I was ready to bring the fight to Matthews. They got too close to achieving what they came out to do. "We will talk about it when we get you downstairs." I told her. Jo and JJ walked in to help them with the bags. Lily came out with my sleeping nephew. She looked exhausted. Shadow and Reap came up to see if we needed any help.

"Hey, one of y'all carry Joyce ass downstairs." T Glen came back up and said. Tank was downstairs loading up the truck with Sincere and Stipes. Shadow was about to pick Ma up but I waved him off. I picked her up and carried her downstairs. Joel was talking to the twins. Whatever she was telling them, had them pissed.

"We want to come with you, Mommy." Mason said to her. Joel looked at him with a stern look.

"I need you to protect your Aunt and your cousins. They need you right now. Your Uncles and father will be there, watching my back, Mason." She told him. Madison grabbed his hand.

"We got this Mommy." She told her. Joel reached down and kissed them both. Kymani and Kymel was standing by the front door waiting for her.

"JJ come get Ma and put her in the car." I asked him. JJ took Ma and walked out with her. I grabbed Joel before she walked out with her brothers.

"Where the fuck are you going?" I asked her. She snatched her arm away from me and tried to walk off again. I snatched her ass up and carried her into the office. She didn't fight me. I speared her brothers a look and they went outside with the rest of the family. I tried to drop her ass, but she landed on her feet. "What the fuck is your problem?" I grilled her.

"Mi nuh ave time to fucking sit here an explain di obvious to yuh." Her voice dropped.

"Joel, we gotta move our family to fucking safety. We are not separating right now." I told her. She threw her head back and laughed.

"Get di fuck outta here. Yuh more dan capable of doing dat. Yuh nuh need mi here holding yuh fucking hand Jason. Get it dun. Mi wi be back soon." She said to me. I knew that she was hurting after hearing what she heard. I calmed myself down and tried to go at her another way.

"I know you are angry, El. But you have to understand, that we need to do this together. Don't shut me out?" I told her. Gage was pacing in front of me like a caged animal. She wanted blood and I didn't blame her. I walked up to her with my hands up. She stopped moving and reached for her blade. "Joel," I called out. "Madison and Mason need us right now. They need their mother and father. We get them to safety and then we will handle our business. I promise you that you will get to torture the fuck outta everyone that was in involved with your mother's death. I promise." I stood in front of her. "You can use the theater." I told her. She stared up at me and held onto my promise. I didn't trust her not to act because she gave in to easily.

Tyja walked in with Callum before I could address it. She looked over at Gage and knew that some shit went down. "It's a go." She told her. Gage turned towards them and her eyes landed on her father. He watched her expression and took a step forward. Gage turned away from him and walked off.

"What happened?" He asked me.

"It's not my place. You would have to talk to Joel." I said and walked past him. I walked outside and got in the car with Joel and the children. I had another spot that I had in mind to put us. It wasn't as big as the apartment building but it was something that they didn't know nothing about. We had to find out how they found us. We were all careful and kept phone conversations short. I knew that Matthews didn't have any connects that could fuck with Tyja and Tristan system.

"I have this cottage house that we could go to. We can cool out there for a few days." Joel's strained voice came through. "The jet is waiting and ready." She said.

"I don't know if that is a good idea. They probably got eyes on the airstrips." I disagreed.

"Don't worry about that. I got that covered." She said. I glanced at her and she was in her angry place. I rolled down my window and motioned for them to follow me. I hoped wherever we were going, was place where she could relax.

9

JOEL

Red. Rage. Anger. And guilt, was what I was feeling. I found myself in my dark place and took a seat. I knew that I wasn't coming out for a while. No matter who was in front me. Not even my children could pull me out of this place. It took everything in me to walk out of the restaurant without putting my hands on her. I didn't want to bless her with a quick death. Oh, I meant what I said. That bitch was going to suffer.

My mother's father, Joel was a farmer in Charlottesville, Virginia. He came to New Orleans to sell some of their fresh produce to some of the famous cooks that were going against each other in the French Quarters cook out. He met my Gammy and never turned back. They lived happily ever after here in New Orleans and raised my mother. When Gramps parents passed away, he left the cottage house to him and the family. When he passed away, he left it to my mom and my mom left it to me. Whenever I needed time to myself, I would go there to relax and regroup.

We pulled up to the fifteen acre land with a six thousand square feet stone cottage house sitting on it. It wasn't that big at first. When I got it, it was only a two bedroom cottage home. I bought more acres around it. We cut down some trees and placed a regular white fence around it. I added on in every year since I got it. It was always an extra bedroom, bathroom, or office that I thought I was going to need. I also had a sunroof in the living area. Mom and I used to like looking up into the sky when we slept. That was why she slept with the window opened. Mom and I came out here for some fresh air. She would wake up and tell me to pack a bag. Once I did, she would drive to the train station and ride all the way up there. My mother was terrified of flying.

Now, I brought the twins out here to do the same. Of course they would do target practice and other weapons training with my brothers. It was a place I thought that will make them feel closer to my mother. When I gave Jason the address to the cottage, the twins cheered. I knew that JoJo reacted the same way, because he loved the horses that we had on the property. Once we pulled up into the long driveway, Jason's eyes was already scanning. He was uncomfortable without all his gadgets and security team. But he had to understand that bringing people around us that we didn't know put us at risk. If Mason didn't catch on to the guy that was pretending to be a guard, they would have succeeded. We were in an open space with some of the deadliest killers. Matthews and Eliria had another thing coming if they thought that they were going to win this battle.

Mason and Madison jumped out the car and ran to the horse stable in the back. JoJo climbed over Jordan to do the same. "Hey! Wait JoJo. We have to see if it is safe." Lily yelled. Kymani walked pass her and walked in the children direction.

"This is the safest place to be, right now." He said. He had been here with Kymel. They knew how much this place meant to me.

"When did you get this, Joel?" Poppa asked looking around the property like everyone else.

"I been had this." I answered him bluntly. I pulled out my keys and walked to the front entrance. Everyone felt the coldness in my voice. On the plane ride here, they kept their distance from me. Kymel and Kymani along with my children and Jason, were the only crazy ones that tried to interact with me. I opened the door and I could have sworn that I could smell my mother's perfume. It was soft and sweet. I walked further in and went straight to the fireplace. Her favorite flowers were still fresh.

"Wow, Joel. I almost forgot how beautiful it is here." Tyja said. I didn't respond back. I just wanted to be alone. I turned and walked down the hall to get to my room. My mother's room was across from mine and locked. I didn't want anyone snooping through her shit. I went in and locked the door behind me. I dropped on the bed and stared up at the ceiling. I replayed the conversation that was had at the restaurant. Eliria told me that her and her brother Antione pretended to be French exchange students. I remember when I got back from Jamaica, Mommy was pushing me to go to France. I told her that I dreamed of living there and dating a famous artist. She found it hilarious, but always told me that anything was possible if I put my mind to it. She gave me pamphlets and all type of shit regarding France. It was an outta the blue subject. She never liked hearing me talk about moving far away from her. She always teased that, she was going to move in my dorm room with me.

She was my best friend. I was able to talk to her about anything. After I killed the men at the house, I talked to her about my training and how hard it was. Mommy tried to help me out by having Kymel or Kymani roll up one of our old mattresses and set up to be a punching bag. She would hold it while I punched and kicked it. We would laugh at how hard she tried to hold on but kept getting knocked off. Kymani and Kymel suggested that they could hold it, but she didn't give up. She supported everything I did. She didn't bother anyone either. That was why it was so hard to understand why Eliria would kill her. They didn't know who I was at the time. Another crazy thing about this was how she knew that I was out of town or where my mother stayed. Poppa was always careful with that. It was something that I had to ask Eliria's ass about. I could ask Poppa but I didn't know if I wanted to hear the answer from him. I mean he did get me to kill my brothers' mother.

I closed my eyes and thought of the many ways that I was going to make her entire family pay. I wanted to go on a major killing spree in France. Anybody that thought that it was smart to work with them assholes was going to die. Slowly and painfully.

I heard my door rattle and then a knock came after. I didn't say anything and got up from the bed. I went into the bathroom and closed the door.

TWO HOURS LATER, I came out of the room. The house was smelling like some smothered cabbage and sweet cornbread with some smothered pork chops. Jason must have asked T Glen to cook my favorite. I walked in the kitchen and everyone was eating and going over some stuff. Jason saw me walking in and got up. He went to the microwave and grabbed a plate of food out of it.

"Come eat, El. You need your energy for what you are about to accomplish." He told me and led me to the table. The children was sitting on the stool at the kitchen island eating there dinner.

"I'm not hungry." I told him and looked at Tyja. "Do you have that for me?" I asked her. She dropped her fork and picked up her napkin to wipe her face.

"Yeah sis. I got that. Are you ready right now?" She asked me. I nodded my head and turned from the table.

"What is it, El?" Poppa asked me again. I kept walking as if I didn't hear him. I heard the chair scrape the floor and knew that he was coming after me. I turned my back to him and didn't acknowledge him at all. Shit was about to get real.

"Mi nuh kno wah di fuck wrong wid yuh but yuh betta get yuh mind right quick, before mi put mi hands pon yuh!" He yelled. I turned and saw that the family followed him. Jason came forward and stood by my side. Madison and Mason grabbed their cousins and went upstairs. They knew that the conversations weren't meant for them. I waited for them to go upstairs to talk to my father. Ma-Ma limped in and sat on the recliner.

"Eliria kill mi mada," I told him out flat. Ma-Ma and T Glen gasped. Tyja had shot up to her chest. Lily leaned in to Jordan, whose mouth was opened with shock. JJ frowned and mumbled under his breath. I didn't expect a reaction from Sincere and Stipes because I just met them, but they did show remorse. Poppa's face went pale grey to a reddish brown in seconds. He was angry. His fist balled up and he swung a right hook into the wall. Kymani had to duck to escape it.

"Wah yuh mean El? Hmm. Shi did tell yuh why? Shi did tell yuh when?" The words barely got through his clenched teeth.

"Shi neva tell mi why but shi did tell mi dat it did round di time dat yuh send mi to kill Vea." I told him while staring at the one man that didn't show any emotions to what I just exposed. I would have thought that he would have been hurt. He was friends with my mother. She used to talk about all the times they shared before I was born. He looked...happy about it.

"Wen yuh meeting up wid them? Dem coming here." He asked.

"Dat a di plan. Shi tell wi dat shi did tire of di cat an mouse game. Dem ready fi di ultimate battle it time dat wi gi it to dem, right Parrain." I said. He smiled at me like a proud father. There was something behind that smile. Jason was looking at him too. He saw what I saw and squeezed my hand. That was another issue that we have to deal with. Poppa walked out of the room and out the house.

It was not too long ago that I found out that he loved my mother. If my mother would have accepted him and all that he did for a living, they would have been together. After hearing when it happened, I knew that he was going to blame himself. Kymel and Kymani looked like they wanted to go and check on him. But they were still pissed at what Poppa did. Now that I knew that he didn't have anything to do with it, I was comfortable with talking to him about it. I knew that he would understand how I felt about all of this. Besides that, I still needed to ask him the question. I let Jason's hand go and walked out after him. Jason was still mugging my Parrain. I hoped that what I was seeing from him was nothing.

I walked out the back door, to my father crying on the back porch. Real tears were rolling down his face. I saw this before. It was the same reaction he showed at my mother's funeral. It was different, though. These were tears of guilt. I sat next to him and grabbed his hand. I waited for him to collect his self and turned towards him to ask him a question. "Yuh kno nuhting bout dis Poppa?"

He turned to face me. Poppa red eyes stared into mine. "Mi neva kno nuhting bout dat baby. Mi love yuh mada. Like mi tell Abigay, yuh mada had mi heart. Mi wudda dun everything inna mi powa to protect har. Everything Joel. Yuh get to believe dat." He said with tears in his eyes. I reached over and wiped his tears away. Eliria was going to pay for these tears. She was going to pay for a lot of shit. I had to find out where she got the information from.

"Papa mi ask yuh who else kno bout mi killing Vea an yuh neva answa mi. There sup'm else dat mi need fi kno bout?" I asked him. He shook his head and dropped eye contact.

"It sup'm dat mi need yuh fi let mi handle. Mi promise yuh dat mi wi tek care of it di way dat wud mek yuh proud." His voice was deeper and unsettling. It sent chills up my spine. Poppa was always a dangerous man. People sometimes forgot about that when he started letting his children do the dirty work. My phone beeped with the information I asked Tyja for.

"Mi haffi mek a run. Yuh cya tell Jason dat mi wud return soon?" I told him after giving him a kiss on the cheek. He looked up at me with concern in his eyes.

"Mi wud like it eff yuh bring sum'ady wid yuh EL. Eff di Eliria knows who yuh dem a guh to try dem best fi get yuh one at a time." Poppa told me standing up.

"Eliria wouldn't wa fi kill mi inna secrecy. Shi wa fi let di whole world kno dat dem betta dan wi. Tyja ave set up a battle ground wid all di assassins inna di world to si. Dem wa wah crowd wi wi gi dem one." I answered. Poppa disagreed and shook his head.

"But Joel eff dat happens, everyone wi kno of yuh identity dem wi cum fi yuh. Mi nuh like dis idea baby." He said to me.

"Dem nuh kno fi wi identity now but fi sum reason dem still coming fi mi an mi fambly. Once dem kno who wi den maybe dem nah fuck wid wi. Mi wi set di example wid Eliria an har brotha's death Di Elites wi ave a face fi di men an women to fear." I told him. He smiled at me like a proud Poppa.

"Call mi wen yuh dun." He told me. I walked out of the side gate and jumped in the car. Tyja set the GPS up to my destination already. Of course, she was totally against this shit, but I had to do something. I was taking a big risk at doing this.

Matthews

I was going to kill these muthafuckers and they knew it. That was why Badrik nor Luis asses never came back to the house. I should've known something was up when they left together. Now Jason and his family left Philly without a trace. After all this was done, I was going to kill them both if Jason didn't do it. We figured that Jason and his family didn't get too far. I was surprised that he was running. The Jason I knew would have met me in the middle of the street to settle this shit. I guess having a family changed shit. Roc checked the Davis' private airstrip and there was no activity.

The guys were packing up our shit for the new location. We also had to travel under the radar. I didn't know who their computer geeks were, but they knew their shit. Roc couldn't uncover shit on Dex's drive which wasn't a surprise. But everything they did after his death, was being hidden and guarded. That was why I got more people to come on board with us. They wasn't as trained as we were but they were doable. More like pawns. Geronimo and Roc were dealing with them because if I had to deal with any more incompetent people, I swear I was going to kill them all.

"We can go to his mother's house to see if there is something that can tell us about where they went." Geronimo said.

"No. There won't be shit there. I don't think that his mother was careless to leave something like that laying around." I told him. A knock on the door interrupted our conversation. Roc picked up his weapon and pointed it at the door. Roc motioned for one of the men to open it. He pulled it and stood on the side for us to see who it was. I took the seat that was facing it and waited for the person to appear. Standing or sitting, I was able to perform the unthinkable.

There was no one in the doorway. This was the type of shit I didn't have time for. Geronimo signaled four men to walk out the door. Before they could reach the door, a white man appeared and yanked the gun out of one of the man's hand disrespectfully. The white man hit the guy with one punch that had him flying back into the wall with a broken neck. Another one of our men tried to rush him, but he was snatched up by his dreads by another white man with a big ass tattoo on his neck. He pulled the man's head down to meet his knee, then yanked the man's dreads out of his head.

The two white men stepped aside and let a white woman with long legs through. I will give it to the new men we had, though. They didn't back down from a fight. After witnessing his friend's death, the third man still charged. He thought that he was going to have a better chance at killing the woman. He ran to her at full speed. Too fast for him to notice, she pulled out her blade and stepped to the side. The blade caught him in the mouth, slicing his head off. The woman cleaned her blade with a handkerchief and placed her blade back into its scabbard. Her moves were swift and quick. She didn't have a piece of hair out of place. Her brothers stared Geronimo and Rock down. The other men stood back, finally using their common sense. Geronimo stepped forward and I held my hand up to stop him. I watched the three of them with calculating eyes. I already knew the ways I wanted to kill them if this unannounced visit went to shit.

"To what do we owe the pleasure?" I asked her. She strolled in and took the seat in front of me. Her brothers walked behind her mechanically and stood behind her.

"Hi Mr. Levy." She said and looked around the room. "I see that you're packing up to leave. Any reason why?" She asked.

"I DON'T THINK what we do on this end concern you. You need to worry about the Elites. That was the only reason why I agreed to let you and your brothers in on this plan. Are you coming to tell me that the job is done?" I asked her. She looked at me and crossed her legs. She was in a sexy nude color suit with some red heels. She was bad but not my type. I liked my women dark and thick.

"No. The job is not done yet." She said with a sigh. "I came across some information that I thought you should know about. It seems that Jason's girlfriend Joel isn't that innocent after all. She and her brothers are the Elites." She told me. I shook my and laughed. I knew that it was something more about her. I just didn't know that it was this big.

"Nothing has changed, Eliria. You still have a job to do." I told her.

"You don't understand. And I think that you are underestimating the situation. I just revealed some information to one of the most lethal killers in the world. Joel is the infamous Gage. She had linked up with another sick muthafucker and she gave birth to their sick ass kids." She told me.

"How do you know that their kids are sick?" Roc asked. She turned her head and looked at him.

"Is he here for show or do you have him here to think? It is just a question. Because the men that attacked us showed what level of intelligence they had." She said.

Roc grunted and moved in her direction. The Hammer dude moved in his path and stared. Eliria laughed and shook her head. "I thought that they taught you guys to have tough skin in the military. My oh my, aren't you sensitive." She said. Eliria turned her head and leaned forward in her seat.

"I got word that it wasn't the Elites that killed your sister. It was their daughter Madison." She continued. I felt the veins in my head throbbing. I knew this bitch didn't say what I thought she said. How could that have been? I heard that Jason's children were only six years of age.

"It's crazy, I know. I would die to have a daughter like that. I guess she couldn't take your sister threatening her father. Same shit happened to me and I lost it. Your sister didn't know the rules. You can't threaten nobody in this game and expect to live. Everyone knows that." She said and shook her head.

"I don't give a fuck about your stupid rules. All I want is Jason and his little bitch's head on a fucking platter." I said and jumped up from my seat. "Where are they?" I grilled her. She looked up at me and batted her eyes.

"We don't know yet. They will be contacting us soon for another "chat". While we have them occupied, you can move forward with your plans. Jason will be left alone with his brothers. I am sure that your well trained men can take them out. But if what is true about Joel's children," she said and pointed to the other men that were in the room. "You are going to need more help."

Eliria stood with her brothers and walked to the door. "I will let you know the location when I am contacted. This will be the only chance you have to get them. Do yourself a favor and don't miss." She said and walked out of the door. Geronimo closed it and waited for me to lose my shit. Roc walked on the opposite side of the room to get out of the line of fire.

I dropped my head back and tried to inhale the air slowly, but I couldn't. I felt uncontrollable. My eyes fell on the men across the room. They didn't understand how fucked they were at that moment. I grabbed the guy that was closer to me and head-butted him in the nose and snapped his neck. I snatched the gun magazine from the table and stabbed the guy that was next to him in the neck. His friend tried to run away but I stopped him with an uppercut elbow to the face. He bent over and held his nose. I grabbed a gun of the table and shot him in the back of the head. The last guy stood with fear in his eyes. He was holding a 45 in his trembling hands. I had no pity for the weak. I pulled my knife from my holster and threw it at his face. It landed right between his eyes. He fell back, hitting the window. I relaxed and waited for myself to cool down. I walked over and pulled the knife out of the man's head.

I looked at Roc and he was waiting for my orders.

"Call up Garnett. Tell him that I need him and his brother here." I told him. I knew that I was losing my fucking mind reaching out to them. They were loose cannons that did whatever they wanted to do. They only thing that I loved about that was they did whatever for the right price. All I had to do was point them in the right direction and they would charge to destroy. Roc sat up and frowned. He wasn't going to voice his opinion because he knew that I didn't give a fuck. He pulled out his phone and dialed the number.

10

JORDAN

We were all sitting and talking about how we were going to get back at Badrik and Luis. Tyja and Tristan had been tracking their whereabouts. The last time we checked, they were still in Philly. We know that they didn't go back to Matthews. They had their own plan and was ready to execute it.

"We can take these two assholes out with no problem, Jason. I can go back to Philly and handle this small problem by myself." Sincere said.

"No, I don't want that to happen. I want us to treat them as the threat that they are. Our children are here." Jason said, which surprised me.

"If that is the case, you could send Mason and Madison after them. You could see how sloppy they were." I said. Jason looked at me and smirked. He knew that his children could have handled all of the men that came for us at the apartment building. I didn't want to put that much pressure on them.

"I know. But I don't want to put them in danger, just like I don't want you two around this shit, Jo." Jason tried again. I speared his ass with a look.

"Don't get your ass beat in front yo friends, Nigga." I told him and stood from the table. He shook his head at the losing battle. I wasn't backing down for shit. That nigga was going to have to knock me out if he didn't want me there.

"Aight, first we gotta try to find out how they knew where we were. Our security system is on point." Tristan said.

"Maybe it wasn't as tight as we thought it was." Sin replied.

"Don't even try it. Our shit is on point. We used Dexter's programming. There was no way that they should have found us." Tyja explained. Kymani and Kymel sat back with Callum and watched the conversation play out. Lily and T Glen were cleaning the kitchen. Ma was upstairs sleeping off pain pills that Joel gave her. Jason was pissed that Joel left without talking to him. You could see that they were going to be moving furniture when she came back. We threw out more ideas and didn't come up with anything that would have kept our family safe. Tristan's computer chimed the same time as the Punisher's phone rang. He looked down at it and walked out the kitchen.

"Yo, J. Come see this." Tristan said. Jason walked to him and looked at the computer screen. "Another one of the pop-up boxes came up. I want to open it but it could be a trap. No one knows that we are here." He said. We all walked to the computer to see what he was talking about.

"Is it from the same server that gave us access to the satellites?" Tyja asked.

"No, it's not." He said and looked up at Jason.

"What are the risks if we open it?" I asked him.

"A lot of fucked up shit. This box is different from the other one. It will give the other server access to everything in my computer, including our location." Tristan told him. Jason shook his head with the rest of us.

"Don't chance." Jason said. The Punisher walked back in the room, while stuffing his phone back in his pocket.

"I just get word from one of mi contacts dat Badrik an Luis inna Jamaica. Him figures dat now dat yuh inna di States, him cya move along wid fi him plan to tek ova Jamaica." He told us.

"Mi nuh worry bout Badrik. Mi cud be inna Hell an him still nah ave a chance to run Jamaica. Mi ave eyes there. Him wi tek care of Badrik eff him sees him." Callum said with dark eyes. Kymani and Kymel smiled at their father.

"Ow yuh get dat fool fi guh back to Jamaica? Him vowed to neva guh back afta meeting fi him wife." Kymani asked.

"Mi tell him bout Cassidy. Him did pissed dat him miss dat an want to mek up fi it." Callum said.

"Dat a gud. Wi should get sum rest. Wi ave been up fi more dat three days." Punisher yawned out.

"Yeah. We all need some rest. We will take turns guarding the house." I told them. Everybody agreed and started disappearing to their room. Tristan sat at the table, staring at the box that kept blinking on his screen.

"What's wrong, T?" Tank asked him.

"Something is telling me to open this box, Bruh. I feel like it is the same person that gave us access to the satellite." Tristan said.

"Dat a di truth but right afta yuh open dat box heavily guard men appear pon fi wi doa step. Listen to yuh cousin." Punisher said and walked out the door.

"I don't think it had anything to do with that." Tristan said.

"Look if the box is still there in the morning, we will open it. But right now, go get you some sleep." Tank told his brother. Tristan rubbed his hand down his face and got up from his chair.

"Aight. Good night." He said and walked out of the kitchen. Tank and I was standing in the kitchen with Jason, Sincere, and Stipes.

"You good, Bruh." I asked Jason. I knew that he wasn't.

"No," he said. The back door opened and in walked Joel. She looked around the kitchen and saw everybody staring at her. Tank and I took a step back waiting for the fireworks to start. Jason surprised us all, by grabbing Joel's hand and walking out the kitchen. "Sincere and Tank got first watch out. Then it will be Stipes and JJ." He told us. Sincere looked pissed.

"What is wrong with you?" Stipes asked.

"I wanted to see her in action. I thought for sure that Jason was about to go off on her. She don't look like the type to take his shit either. I saw that when they came down to New Orleans. She had his ass eating out her hands." He told us and we all laughed. We saw how much she changed him for the best. She was the real MVP.

"I'll be back. I am going to go get my charger." Tank said while answering his phone and walked out of the kitchen. I was about to do the same but Stipes stopped me.

"Yo, Jordan. Can we talk to you for a minute?" He asked me.

"Yeah, what's up?" I replied. He leaned on the kitchen island and looked over at me.

"You know that your brother isn't an easy person to get along with. When we met him, he didn't want to be bothered. He stayed to his self and kept it moving, no matter what. With each mission, we got closer and gained each other's trust. Stipes and Jason are the only two men that I trust with my life. I wanted to stay enlisted. I told your brother and he told me that he had a bad feeling about the crew that they were sending me with. I declined and resigned. I didn't question him because it had been times when he was right on about what he felt. Three weeks later, the crew was killed by a suicidal bomber. I thanked him every day of my life, Man. He wasn't telling you to sit it out because he thought you couldn't hang. He was telling you that because he is worried. I have been around this family for a couple of days and I see the bond that these niggas fight over. Y'all may have had troubled times, but it brought you together stronger. You got to understand that he is doing whatever he has to do to keep that bond and that trust the rest of you have in him. If he makes one wrong decision, it will cause more than your life but the life of your family, too." Sincere told me.

"I understand, Bruh. I just cannot not be there for him. Neither can JJ. We have been through a lot. I don't want to let him down again." I said truthfully. Stipes walked over to me and put his hand on my shoulder.

"Listening to your brother won't be you letting him down. It would be showing him that you trust him." Stipes told me. "See you at midnight." He said to me and went to bed. I nodded at Sincere and went to my room. I had to reevaluate some shit before I came up with a decision.

Jason

I PULLED her in the room and locked the door. Her ass had been gone for two and a half hours without a phone call. I thought that she needed time, but with everything that was going on she needed to stay in contact with one of us. Me in particular. I turned to go off on her ass. Joel pushed me into the door and slammed her lips on mine. She pulled and sucked on my tongue, while pulling down my basketball shorts. When my shorts were down to my ankles, she dropped down to her knees and stuff my entire length into her mouth.

"What the fuck, El?" I groaned out and held onto the wall. I felt my eyes rolling in the back of my head. Joel started humming and massaging my sack. She slurped and pumped. Pumped then slurped. She was working my shit like she was auditioning to be a porn star.

"El, stop Bae." I rushed out. I felt myself getting close but her ass never listened. She thought that it was funny to have me climbing the fucking walls. I grabbed a fistful of her hair and tugged. She locked her jaws and swallowed my shit. "ELLLL! Fuck!" I yelled out. She ignored me again and continued with her mind blowing head. Fuck that shit. I wasn't going to be no punk and bust quick like this. I snatched her ass up and threw her ass on the bed. I stepped out of my shorts and watched her peel herself out of those tight ass jeans. I got to the bed and ripped off her shirt and bra. She gave me that dark lustful look. The "anyway you want it" look. *Fuck.*

I grabbed her legs and pulled her to the edge of the bed. I got on my knees and placed my tongue on its holder. I wrapped my tongue around her sinful nub and tugged. "Nuh stop love." She moaned out. I loved when she talked that shit to me. Mind you, at times, I didn't understand what she was saying. But I grasped on to the main words and made sense out of that shit. I didn't bother trying to understand that shit during sex. I wanted her to repeat the shit over and over.

She grabbed my ears and grind her pussy on my tongue. Baby girl was moaning and screaming my name in six different languages. That shit turned me on even more. I nibbled on her button and watched my pussy overflow with the sweetest treat I have ever had. Her legs were wrapped tightly around my head. I pulled her legs loose and watched the love in her eyes. She opened her legs wider and grabbed my ears to pull me down. I grabbed her legs and slid into the gates of heaven.

"Damn El. This shit feels so good, Bae." I told her. She started sucking on my neck and rotating her hips.

"Fuck mi harda, Jason. Mek yuh pussy cum." She moaned. I didn't want to disappoint her. I pulled her off the bed while I was still inside of her. I stood on my feet and wrapped her legs around me.

"Harder?" I asked her to make sure that was what she wanted. She pulled herself up an bit my lip as the answer. I nodded and smirked at her. "Hold on." I told her. I pushed her body back and pulled it towards my body hard.

"Ahh. Ohhh, J!" She screamed. I did it again and she wrapped her arms around my neck. She sat up higher on my waist and began to go up and down on my dick like she was on a horse. Joel was riding the shit out of me. We stared into each other's eyes before releasing a mind blowing orgasm. I turned and fell on the bed with her on top of me. We both were breathing like we ran ten miles. She sat up and looked at me with her sweet Joel eyes. "Do you trust me?" She asked. I pushed her hair out of her face and grabbed the back of her neck.

"Yes, I do." I answered.

"You know that I will do anything for you, right." She said.

"Yeah, I know. Why are you telling me this?" I asked her. She kissed me and smiled.

"When the time comes, I need you to know that. I need you to know that you trust me and that I have your best intentions in mind." She said. I didn't want to ask her another question about what she said, because I didn't want her to think that I didn't trust her. I pulled her down and wrapped my arms around her. I closed my eyes and was about to get the peaceful sleep that Joel's loving promised me. That didn't happen with Tristan ass knocking on our door frantically.

"Jason. Open the door man. Hurry the fuck up and open the door." He said in a harsh whisper. I jumped up and threw my boxer briefs and basketball shorts on. Joel rolled out of the bed and went to the bathroom. I opened the door and this nigga looked spooked.

"What the fuck is wrong with you?" I asked him. He walked in with his laptop and sat it on the dresser in the room.

"I know you told me not to click on the box, but something was telling me to do it, J. Once I clicked on it, this was what pulled up." He said. I looked at the screen and saw that Badrik and Luis where on their way to the house. It looked like they were ten miles away from the house.

"Wake up JJ and Jordan. Don't be loud about it." I told him. He walked out of the room to do what I asked him. "El put some clothes on, Sweetheart. We are going hunting." I told her. I took off my shorts and put on some black sweats with a black shirt and J's. Joel came out with some black jeans and sweater. She let her hair loose and strapped up her boots. We walked out of our room and into the kitchen. Sincere and Tank were checking their weapons. Kymani, Kymel, and Callum walked out with black jeans on and nothing else. Those niggas blended in with the night. The rest of us had to wear black to blend in. Punisher walked out with that big ass knife that the Indian had on the first Predator.

"Alright. I don't want them making it to this house. There is only one road that they can come from. But I want us to cover all angles." I told them.

"Dat wi be fine. Di Elites an Punisha wid mi. Di rest wid yuh. Tristan cud stay pon di coms just inna case him si sup'm different. Tank stay wid Tristan." Callum suggested. I didn't like that shit. Gage looked at me and shook her head.

"It nuh di fucking time," she growled and pulled out her knives. She walked to the breaker box that was in the room and shut off the lights. We took the front, while they took the back. Jo and Stipes flanked my right, while Sincere and JJ had my left. I saw the four trucks coming up the road. My brothers spread out and left me in the middle of the road. I stood there and waited for the truck to get closer. Once it did, the driver turned on the high beams. I stared through the glass and saw Luis' stupid ass in the passenger seat. Like the dummy I knew him to be, he got out the car and walked my way.

"So you are Jason. The muthafucker that ruined my family's life. I didn't think that you would have made it this easy to kill you." He said with a gun in his hand. I didn't say nothing. I waited for the right time to show my cards. Because if he was anything like his bitch ass daddy, he was going to keep talking.

"And you are?" I pretended.

"I know you know who I am and why I am here." He said while raising the gun at the house. "And when I am done with you, I will make sure that your children lives a lifetime of slavery to my buyers. Do you know how much I could get for Jason Davis' children? It will set my children up for life." He bragged. I felt my blood rising but I had to maintain my cool. It was almost time.

"Even if you do get through me, my children won't be easily taken. I'm going to need you to know that. It will be best if you die right here." I said while flexing my wrist. Luis started laughing and talking that Spanish shit.

"You and your family ain't shit. I will sell your daughter to the highest bidder and make sure that she is nice and ripe for them. I have a few people in mind that would test that. Your son will never see the light of day again. I will put him in dungeon. The same place that my father died." He almost shouted at me.

I smiled knowingly. I knew that they would come. I heard their footsteps while he was talking that shit. I saw movement by the car. The high beams switched off and my brothers were standing there watching Luis' rant. Luis turned around and saw that the men that he came with were dead. He didn't have the same courage as he did before. I saw the bead of sweat forming on his forehead. He looked at my brothers and took a step back. I hated muthafuckers like him. They talked that shit when there were a lot of people backing them, but bitched up when they got by themselves. Sincere stepped forward to get first dibs on beating his ass. JJ held him back and nodded his head. Sincere and Stipes frowned at us. They were trying to figure out why I didn't kill him. I shook my head and walked towards a shivering Luis.

"You are just like yo punk ass Daddy. Instead of shooting me, like any of us would have done. You ran your fucking mouth and got caught up." I told him. "When I first heard that it was you that was with Matthews, I knew that I was going to be the one to kill you. But then I realized, this isn't my fight. You didn't join the Matthews' crew to kill me. You did it to kidnap my children." I laughed while thinking about. "This is their fight. And I always believe in letting them fight their own battles." I told him and felt my children standing on the side of me. Mason was standing with his blade, tapping it on his leg. Madison stared at him with hate and anger. She had her small knives in her holster belt.

"Nuh worry fada wi wi mek sure dat Mr Luis goes out inna style," Mason growled. Luis looked down at them and almost smiled.

"What type of father are you? You put your children in danger like this." He asked. Madison stepped forward and sneered at him.

"Mi padre es el mejor. A diferencia de usted. Pensabas que iba a casa vivito y coleando, por lo que no besas a tus hijos adios. La espalda será su última memoria de ustedes." She told him in Spanish. She wanted him to understand everything that she was saying. We all saw the surprise on his face, hearing Madison talk in his native tongue. I walked backwards to the guys. JJ and Jo sat on the hood of the truck, while Sincere and Stipes moved in front of the car. Luis looked at me and started laughing. He thought that he had it covered. "Si eso es lo que quieres jugar a los niños. Sólo quiero hacerle saber que quiero que sostiene detrás." He said and tossed his gun, which was the dumbest shit to do ever.

"Estás de suerte. Tampoco nos va." Mason told him and went straight for his ankles with the blade. He jumped out of the way, like his feet were on hot coal. He grabbed Mason's hand and tried to lift him. Madison snatched two knives from her belt and threw them at his hand.

"Oww you bitch." He yelled and let Mason go. That gave Mason a chance to slice through his main vein. Luis raised his hand to hit Mason and was stopped by another knife that Madison threw. He yanked it out of his arm and started walking towards Madison. She didn't move. She waited for him to get close and went into her other holster and to grab her knuckle knife. Luis went to swing on her. She dodged it and punched up into his extended arm. She stepped on the side of him and punched him on the side of his right knee. He dropped and was now eye level to his makers.

Mason walked behind him with his brass knuckles in his hand. Without looking at each other, they punched him in the head at the same time. We watched as they beat him to a pulp. Sincere moved to get a closer view. He didn't believe what he was seeing. Stipes shook his head and smiled. "Yeah, Gage gotta be they Mama." He said fucking with me. I didn't say nothing back.

My children stepped back and watched Luis fall back on the ground. Mason walked up and stood over him. Luis was coughing up blood and tried to open his closed eyes to see him. "This will be the dungeon that you promised me. Slowly dying out here, alone with no one or nothing to save you. My sister and I will live the life that your children could have. A one with a father. Your vengeance will be the reason that they will get older and come for us. And when they do, we will be ready to send them to you." Mason told him. He grabbed his sister's hand and walked to us. Mason looked up at me for the approval that I knew he was looking for.

"You did great son. I'm proud of you. The both of you." I told them and dapped a smiling Mason off.

"Thank you, Daddy." Madison said in the sweet voice that we all loved. I picked her up and kissed her on the cheek.

"You're welcome Angel. I need you guys to go back into the house, before your mother tries to kill me." I told them. They both laughed and walked back to the house. JJ shook his head at me.

"You know damn well that she don't have to try." He said. We heard shots coming from the back of the house. The children looked back at me. "Go into the horse's stable." I told them. They took off in that direction as the rest of us followed the shots.

Once we got there, we saw heads and other body parts, scattered around the property. The shit looked like a wild animal was attacking people out here. Callum and the Punisher was working on five men, while the Elites were running through the other group easily. We stayed back and watched them kill with precise moves. It looked like they were creating art out here. Some men ran our way and we had no problems with taking them down. I saw Gage running deeper in the woods after someone. Shadow followed her. I didn't fuck around with the guy that I was supposed to fight. I pulled out my gun and shot him in the head twice. I ran full speed after Gage. I knew that she was a killer but it still didn't stop me from worrying about her.

I heard the men grunting and blows being landed. I walked up and saw Gage standing on the side as Kymel went to work on Badrik. Kymel was swinging right and left hooks. They were so fast that Badrik thought he was getting jumped. Kymel hit that nigga with one swift kick to the stomach and had that boy falling to his knees. Badrik held his hand up to stop Kymel from his final blow.

"Eff fada did there fi mi like him did there fi unu dis shit wouldn't be like dis. Yuh ave mi empire. Yuh an yuh sick ass siblings nuh deserve di shit dat did given to yuh. Mi did haffi wuk fi get weh mi deh at without fada. All mi want did to be accept." He said. I wanted to say something badly, but Kymel beat me to it.

"Shut yuh fucking crying bowy, an tek yuh whipping like a man. Yuh come fi mi an mi fambly an now looking fi sum'ady to feel sorry fi yuh. There ave been many men dat did raise without dem fada an come up di way yuh did. All yuh did haffi duh did to stay yuh distance. Mi fada an sista warn yuh mada an shi neva listen. No more warnings." Shadow told him. Badrik shook his head and his eyes went to Joel. Callum and Reap walked up with Punisher. They stood and watched the shit that was going on.

"Yaah guh let dem kill mi Fada." Badrik asked. I thought that he was talking to God. Because we already established that Callum was not his father. I looked over at Joel and saw a gun pointed to her head. I stepped towards her and the hoe ass nigga cocked the gun back. Her family didn't look shocked at all. They could have prevented it.

"Back up Kymel." Punisher said. Shadow looked back at him and shook his head.

"Mi nuh believe dis shit." Shadow said, but didn't back up.

"Believe it an back yuh ass up. Badrik get p an guh a wuk." Punisher said. Badrik got up and took his shirt off. He had all types of skulls tatted on his body. He started stretching and bouncing up and down. In a matter of minutes, he didn't look like the same weak muthafucker before. He looked trained. Gage smirked at him.

"Eff yuh using mi as leverage, yuh might as well kill mi. Mi nuh a guh watch yuh piece of a sit son beat pon mi bredda." Gage said.

"Mi wud neva kill yuh baby." Punisher whispered. He kept his eyes on Callum and Reap. Callum eyes shot fire into the Punisher's. He knew that he wasn't going to live after this. Shadow squared off and went at Badrik hard. Badrik blocked his shots and landed a few of his own. Everything that Shadow did, Badrik knew before hand and landed hard body shots. Shadow winced at one and stepped back. Shadow must have told that nigga about the Elites' methods. There was no way for him to know what Shadow was going to do.

Shadow rotated his neck and changed his style of fighting. Badrik's ass looked shook. Shadow lit his ass up with some kicks and pressure point hits. It was the same method that the children used on him. I guess Punisher didn't teach him this because his ass was lost. Badrik looked over at Punisher and tried to get help, but it was no use. In that moment, Shadow hit that boy with the special punch. Badrik flew back and slid on the ground. He started gasping for air and reaching out to the Punisher. Shadow walked off and stood next to the family while Badrik took his last breath.

"Mi neva teach yuh dat. Dat did ongle fi Joel to kno." Punisher said.

"Yeah, she teach mi." Shadow said with anger in his eyes. The family have been betrayed by a man that help raised them to be what they are now. No matter how hard she tried, Gage couldn't hide the hurt in her eyes. Callum stepped forward and asked the question that we all wanted to know.

"Why," he asked through clenched teeth.

"Because she was mine and you took her from me." He said in perfect English. Shadow and Reap eyes bunched up. They were confused about his answer. Punisher walked around Joel with the gun in her face. He stared at her with the type of love that you would see a father show.

"I met your mother first in New Orleans. We talked and got to know each other. And after the many conversations we had, I knew that she was going to be the one for me. I told your father about her and wanted him to meet her. I wanted to know what he thought of her. He saw her and felt the same thing I felt. The difference between the two was that he didn't try to get to know her. He only wanted the one thing that I waited for. She called me the night she threw his ass out and asked about what Callum told her. You see your mother didn't know what type of work I did. I told her that I was a travel businessman. Callum stupid ass felt the need to tell her the truth about our work for whatever reason. She decided that she didn't want to deal with any of us anymore. I tried to call her or pass by, but she ignored me.

Callum called me a few weeks after and told me that she was pregnant. I was so pissed that I took the next flight out there and confronted her. She told me that it was true and started crying. I tried to get her to run away with me, but she told me no. She didn't want to leave her home for no one. I gave up on her. And then you came. You were the perfect daughter. I told Callum that I was going to train you to be the best killer alive. And that I did. You were feared by many at the age of twelve." He said.

"What about Badrik? How that happened?" Reaper asked. Punisher answered him without removing his eyes from Gage.

"When your Callum started messing Cassidy, I came back in a fit of rage and fucked Abigail. She was pregnant around the same time as Cassidy. That was why she thought that the baby was for Callum. He fucked her before he came to meet Cassidy. When Callum told me about the baby not being his, I knew that Badrik was mine. Abigail didn't want to admit to it, but I knew. Once he was older I told him the truth. He didn't like it but he accepted it and asked me for a favor. He wanted Callum's empire and I was willing to snatch what he loved the same way he did me." He said.

"It was you that leaked where we were. It didn't have anything to do with that pop-up box." I said. He nodded his head. Joel stepped forward and grilled him.

"You did all that for what? In the end, you still didn't tell your son who we truly were. You fought next to us and watched him die. What was the reason for all of this?" Joel said coming down from her high.

"I couldn't let them kill my daughter." He mumbled. Callum took a step forward this time and placed his self in front of the gun.

"She is not yours, muthafucker. She is my fucking daughter. It ain't in you to make someone like her." Callum told him. Punisher stepped back and placed his finger on the trigger this time.

"She is mine. Everything that she does, it is because of me. I told Cassidy that. I told her that we can make more like Joel if she gave me a chance. But no, she was waiting on your dumb ass like you were some fucking prize. You didn't love her like I did. I wasn't going to let you have her! You didn't deserve her!" He yelled. And that was when the atmosphere changed. It went from a warm to a chilly night. I looked at Joel and saw the tears pooling in her eyes.

"It was you," she said as if the words were stuck in her throat. Callum tilted his head to the side and waited for him to answer. Punisher looked behind Callum and into his God-daughter's eyes.

"She was mine." He said. "I loved her. She told me that she didn't want to be with me. When I tried to kiss her, she pushed me back and picked up her a vase and pitched it at me. I tried to apologize, but it was too late. She told me to get out and never come back. I called Abigail and told her the information she needed for Eliria to do the job." Punisher told her. Callum yelled out in a fit of rage and attacked Punisher. Callum hit Punisher with a vicious blow. He stumbled back and recovered slowly. Callum didn't rush it either. He was going to make Punisher pay.

Punisher dropped the gun and reached back to pull out that big ass knife. Joel tossed her blade at her father right before he swung down on him. They were out here swinging those fucking blades like they were Samurais. Punisher's blade came down on Callum's arm. He escaped the full blow but was cut. It didn't stop him, though. The adrenaline that was pumping in his veins had him going harder and moving faster.

Callum swung the blade like a bat, throwing Punisher off. The impact of that swing had Punisher's blade flying to the left. The Punisher looked at Callum and waited for his final words. It didn't come. Callum swung the blade and cut his head off. The head dropped on the ground and Callum stabbed it with the blade. He picked it up and carried it back to the house with him. He walked past us without speaking a word. Joel was staring at the body on the ground. Kymani was on the phone with their cleanup crew. I walked and stood by Joel's side.

"I knew that he had something to do with it. When I told Poppa who killed her, he didn't look surprised. It looked like he was happy." She whispered. I grabbed her hand and pulled her away from the scene.

"It's going to be alright, El." I told her the only thing that could come to mind. There was nothing to say in a situation like this. I just needed her to understand that I was there for her however she needed me to be. She leaned on my shoulder and continued walking to the house. Hopefully, we could really get some rest now before Matthews find our location.

11

JOEL

I was mentally and physically drained. Poppa didn't confirm or say shit about what was said a day ago. He was quiet for the rest of our time at the house. I didn't know how to feel about the shit. My brothers tried to make sense of it too, but we got nowhere. And that shit was frustrating. On top of all that, we got information that we were supposed to meet with Eliria and her brothers on the next day. I wasn't cool with that. I asked the cleanup crew to bury the bodies of the men in the back yard. I was going to plant trees over their bodies. It was going to be the true form of your haters throwing shade.

Jason and I talked to the children about them staying close the house. We didn't want them to join this fight at all. They didn't pout like I thought they would. JJ and Jo were still hell bent on coming with us as well. Jason didn't try to talk them down again. He was going to stay by their side just in case shit popped off. I was sitting with the women of the family and reminiscing on everything that we had been through. The birth of the children, the death of Pops, and the men that we were all in love with. Tristan came out and told T Glen that she was going to be a Grandmother. She surprised him by telling that she knew already.

"How you knew, Ma? I knew that Jason or Tristan didn't tell you." He asked her.

"Yo ass was sleeping and that stupid phone kept ringing. I answered it and I talked to April. She told me that she was pregnant two weeks ago." She told him.

"Ma, I told you about answering my phone." Tank said. "You lucky you didn't see the pictures in there." He told her.

"I know that your dumb ass don't have that pornographic shit in your phone. You a filthy muthafucker." T Glen said and walked out. We all started laughing. JJ came in there and whispered something into Tyja ear. Her crazy ass jumped from her seat and followed him out the kitchen door. Ma-Ma smiled.

"I am going to have more grandbabies." She said. We all knew that, that was going to be true. Lily was shaking her head like they weren't going to come from her. Jordan was a Davis man, just like Joseph and Jason. Jason was talking all that shit about me being on birth control. Tyja told me that Joseph hid her pills, but how her hot ass was running out the kitchen, she didn't have any objections.

"Hey, when did you teach Kymel the special hit?" Kymani asked. I turned and saw that he was standing in the middle of the doorway. Poppa had my old neighbor Malcolm run his businesses while we out here. Mani gave his phone to Tristian to fix. Instead of that, Tristan found out that the two women he was fucking with worked for Luis. Malcolm went to Kymani's house to kill the women. They were waiting for Kymani to get back.

"I taught him that some years ago. He took him almost seven months to learn it." I said.

"When are you going to show me?" He asked me. I shook my head.

"I am not teaching you that shit Reap. You play too much. You would do some shit like that to us, off guard just because. No." I told him. He hunched his shoulders, knowing that I was telling the truth. Sin called out for us to go to the office. My brothers and I went into the office with the Davis crew and his Seal brother. Jason gave us the information that we needed for the trip to Eliria. Kymel looked over at me and yawned. I tried not to laugh, but this was how Jason planned for shit. We on the other hand went on impulse. I didn't have time to issue out orders to other people. They'd fuck up and then get me killed. Poppa walked through the door and waited for Jason to finish. "I think that it will be best if we move. Rajae could have told them where we are. If that is the case, while we are at the meeting." He told us.

"If that was the case, I think that they would have been here by now." Kymani said. Poppa turned and looked at him.

"That may be true, but I want us to be safe than sorry." He said and walked out the room. I was done with the running. I trusted Jason to keep everyone safe while we dealt with Eliria. I got up and walked behind him. He went to his room and started packing.

"Poppa, I don't think that we should move. If push comes to shove, you can stay here with them and help if there is an attack." I told him. He stopped with his clothes in his hands and glared up at me.

"Can you tell me the real reason why you don't want to leave this place?" He asked me. I moved his clothes out of the way and sat on the bed. I took in a deep breath before speaking.

"Mom used to bring me here." I told him. He nodded his understanding and sat next to me.

"I feel her here with me sometimes. That gives me strength." I whispered. Poppa grabbed my hand and kissed it.

"Dat did ow shi make mi feel." He said and sighed. "Mi nuh kno El. Mi nuh kno wah to tink anymore. Mi hate dat yuh mada neva tell mi bout Rajae an fi him advances. Mi wudda kill fi him ass a lang time ago." He said.

"And that was probably why she didn't tell you. She wanted you out Poppa. If she would have told you what happen, she would have felt like she was contributing bodies for you to kill. She loved you that much." I told them.

"An mi love har back." He said while staring in my eyes. I saw nothing but the truth. I reached out and hugged my father tightly. I knew that he seen shit in his life that was going to be hard for him to get over. But in the past few days, he was struggling.

"What you ladies have planning on cooking?" He asked me. I pulled back and smile.

"Oxtails and jerk chicken." I told him. Poppa eyes lit up and rubbed his stomach. I knew the way to this killer's heart was food. Poppa loved a woman that could throw down in the kitchen. We got up and walked back to the kitchen. T Glen and Lily was making plates while Ma-Ma and Madison was setting the table. Tyja was holding a sleeping Jerimiah. "You need to put that baby down before you spoil him." I told her.

"Girl please. He already spoil." She said while rocking him. JJ was staring at her. I wondered if he told her how he felt because that shit was written all over his face. Mason was play fighting with Jason in the living area. Matter of fact, all the men were lounging on the floor playing cards and that made me come up with an idea.

"Hey guys, how about we have a nice picnic in the living area?" I asked.

"Yeah that sound like a good idea." Lilly said. The kids were excited about it, but the men looked skeptical.

"What's wrong with that idea?" Ma-Ma asked.

"Nobody don't want to sit on the floor and eat. That is why we got tables." Kymel's stupid ass said. I shot a glare his way.

"Get up and move the furniture back." I told him. He poked his tongue out at me and did what I asked. Jason winked at me and helped the rest of the guys move some furniture to the other room. Mason and JoJo went to get some blankets to place them on the floor. We started to bring the food in and placing them in the middle of the blanket. We had some greens, mac n cheese, and cornbread with the oxtails and jerk chicken. We all sat down and ate. Jason got up and went to get his MP3 speakers. He turned on some music and that had everyone rocking. The children got up and started doing the newest dances. We laughed and was enjoying the time that we all could spend with each other. "Hey do anyone want anything else." I asked them.

"Yes. Some greens, Bae." Jason told me. I kissed his lips and stood with the serving bowl. I walked into the kitchen and lights flashing through the kitchen window caught my attention. I walked to it with caution. I peeked out the window and saw guns pointed at the house. *Here we go*, I thought. I heard the first gun clicked.

"Everyone stay down!" I yelled and hit the floor. No sooner than I did, bullets started flying through the house. I crawled my way back to the living room. Jo was covering his family. JJ had Ma-Ma and Tyja. T Glen was covered by Tristan. Poppa had Madison and Mason. Tank rolled over to the other side of the room and began tossing guns to Jason and my brothers. I moved the blanket and called out to Mason.

"Mace press it." I told him. He nodded his head and made his way to the fireplace. There were some other rooms I added while I was redesigning the house. A panic room was one of them. Mason pressed the button. A piece of the floor board popped up. I pulled on it and slid it back and stairs appeared.

"Jordan! This way!" I yelled for him. He turned my way and saw our exit strategy.

"JoJo. I want you to crawl to your Aunt Joel, ok. Can you be a big boy for me and do that?" He asked him calmly. JoJo nodded his head and crawled to me with no problems. Lily stood on her feet and duck walked to me. When she got to the stairs. JoJo was reaching out for his little brother.

"Give him to me Mom." He shouted over the gunfire. Lily placed Jerimiah in his hand. JoJo began to walk down the stairs into a nicely built fort. It looked like a huge studio apartment down there. It was good that Lily passed Jerimiah off, because she needed two hands to get down there. Ma-Ma and T Glen was next. When they got down there, someone kicked the door open. I slid the door shut and motioned for Tyja to get behind the sofa. Tank passed Tristan a gun and placed him behind him.

"You stay behind me Tristan. Don't get all brave, Nigga." He told him. Tristan nodded his head. You can tell that he wasn't comfortable about the situation. JJ was guarding the sofa like it was on sale on Black Friday. A man appeared and pointed his gun towards us. Jordan blasted his ass with a sawed off. The men started piling in and we were killing them as they appeared. I looked up and saw that there were men on the roof. I shot up and hit two of them. One of them fell off the roof, while the other fell into the house through the sunroof.

I rolled out the way before he landed. I grabbed his gun and started shooting. "We got to lead them away from everyone." Kymani said. I was cool with that but I had my children out here. There were calm and sat with Tyja behind the sofa.

"We got to find a place for Tyja and the children. I am not going hunting knowing that they are in the opening." I told him. Poppa moved forward.

"I will take them. You go and help the rest of them." He told me and went to them. The gunfire stopped. That gave us some time to get our weapons and prepare for the next wave. JJ looked back at the couch where Tyja was. She looked at him and smiled. He mouthed that he love her and at that moment a bullet came through the window and hit him in the chest.

"NOOOOOOO!" Tyja yelled and tried to get to JJ.

Poppa held her back the best way he could. Tyja struggled in Poppa arms. He had to press on one of her pressure points to calm her down. Jason and Jo looked back. Jo ran over to check on him and was hit in the back by another bullet. He fell to his knees and gasped for air. He turned his head and looked at Jason. Jason moved to get to them, but Sincere held him down. Tristan and Tank were looking at their cousins lying on the floor. Tristan held his gun up higher and was now ready to take out some lives.

Tank waited for Jason to lose his shit because he was ready to go out with him. The bullets started up again, but not as many as before. I could tell that we took majority of their crew out. I saw Mason peeked around the couch and saw that his Uncles were shot. He made eye contact with me. The tears in his eyes was for JoJo.

"AHHHHH!" Jason bellowed out. I ran to him and grabbed his face. "Listen, I know that you are hurt right now. But you have to maintain your cool. This is what Matthews want. He wants you reckless and careless. He thinks that, that is the only way to beat you. You still have your family to protect. We will grieve but not now. Stay focused, Baby. Trust me and stay focused." I told him, but I don't think that I was getting through. This was the Jason that I saw when his father died.

Jason looked at me with dead eyes. The pain in them will be something that I won't forget. I caressed his face and tried again. "Wi wi kill every laas one of dem. Tell wi wah yuh need wi to duh Jason." I asked with my dead eyes showing. He looked at me now.

"I want the sniper." He said with hell behind those words. I nodded my head.

"An him yuh should ave." I told him and wiped the tears from his eyes. I turned back at my Kymani. "Ow many out there." I asked him. He crawled to the window and stuck his head up quickly.

"Three of dem. Four wid di snipa." He answered.

"Did you see the sniper?" Stipes asked.

"No. There a one inna di middle. Two of dem pon each side of di yaad." Kymani answered. The shooting stopped with a man screaming.

"Kill them kids." I heard someone yell. Without thinking, I jumped out the window towards the shooting. Jason was already out the front door. We looked and saw our daughter on top of a man. She stabbed him and pressed the button on the handle of the knife. The body blew up and she rolled off him, ready for the next one. Mason was fighting with one of Jason's Seal brothers, Roc. He dodged hits and was hit with two blows to the chest. He grabbed his chest and spit out blood. Madison was running towards and Geronimo caught her by the hair.

Sincere came from out of nowhere and tackled Geronimo to the ground with Madison. She rolled out of the way and tried to get to her brother. Matthews pulled out his gun and shot towards her. She dodged the first three bullets. The fourth one grazed her shoulder and she went down. I pulled out a knife to throw at him and felt someone grab my hand.

"You smell like you got a pretty pussy." A man whispered in my ear. I dropped the knife in my other hand and turned in the man arm, slicing his stomach. I stepped back and pulled another knife out of my holster and threw it behind me without looking. The man that grabbed me was a black, bald-headed man. He grabbed his stomach and smiled at the pain that I knew he was in. "Was that supposed to tickle?" He asked.

"Oh yuh wa fi laugh muthafucka." I heard Reap say. The man looked at him and shook his head.

"I ain't gay nigga. I want to have this dance with her." He said.

"No tank yuh. Mi nuh ave time to teach yuh di steps. Reap." I said and turned to see about my child. Mason was holding onto her as Roc and Stipes fought. I ran by their side and dropped to my knees. Madison had blood coming from her shoulder, but I was happy that it was nothing that she couldn't recover from. "I will talk to you two later. Right now. We gotta get your sister in the house." I told them. Tank and Tristan came from around the house with blood spattered on their clothes. Shadow walked up to us and looked at Madison's shoulder.

"Which muthafucka did it?" He asked. I pointed towards Matthews. The knife I threw was sharp enough to cut the gun in half. He was now starring Jason down. Sincere caught Geronimo with an uppercut that had him hitting the tree behind him. Sincere took his head and rammed it in the tree over and over again. Stipes had Roc in a submission hold. He squeezed his leg around Roc's neck and snapped it. Matthews was the only one standing. I knew that Jason would have killed any of us if we jumped in the fight between the two. Jason rotated his neck and threw a quick punch. Matthews blocked it and countered with a hit of his own. It landed on Jason's face, hard. Matthews swung again and missed. Jason caught him by the neck and swept his feet from under him. Then he slammed Matthews to the ground.

Jason hit him with body shots and two to the dome. Matthews caught the next punch and locked Jason's wrist under his arm. He pulled Jason's head closer to his and head-butted him twice. Matthews kicked Jason off him and jumped up. I could see how dizzy he was from that hit. He staggered and fell on his knees. I stood and was ready for the backlash that he was going to give me. What I wasn't going to do is stand here and watch him get kill. Kymani got to us and snatched my ass up.

"He got this." He told me.

I looked back and saw that Matthews was walking towards him. Jason had his head down. Matthews got closer and tried to kick him. Jason grabbed his leg and placed it on his shoulder. He pulled the leg down and it cracked.

"ARGH!" Matthews yelled and tried to punch him. Jason took that arm and snapped that too and punched him in the mouth. Matthews fell to the ground. Jason stood up and waited for Matthews to collect himself. He tried to stand but kept falling. He chuckled and spat out blood. "I thought that you were like me. I saw it in your eyes. I should've killed you when I had a chance." He told him. He pulled an old flip phone. "Like I told you before, none of us should be breathing. We are the black clouds that blocks the sun from shining on the people that should be growing." He held up the phone with his other hand.

"Shit. That's a fucking detonator!" Sincere shouted. Matthews pressed the button and nothing happened. We all looked around and waited for something to blow up. We saw a figure walking up to us with something in his hand.

"I hope you didn't think that it was going to be that easy." Dex said. Matthews didn't look surprised.

"I should have known that you were still alive. You made it too easy." He told him.

"And that is why you will never win." Dex said and looked at Jason. He threw a weapon to Jason. It was the shotgun that had his something filed on it. He aimed it at Matthews' face and let off two shots. Matthews' face was no more.

"Where the fuck have you been?" Sincere asked Dex. Dex walked up to them and dapped everyone off.

"I was there for y'all. All the pop-up boxes and shit. That was me leaving y'all little breadcrumbs." Dex said. Jason walked up to us and handed the weapon back to Dex. Sincere looked at the weapon and smiled.

"I didn't know that you kept Flex's weapon." He told Dex.

"Yeah. This was the one that had his kids name on it. I couldn't let them give this one away." Dex told him.

"Good looking out." He told Dex. Dex looked at Jason and knew that something was wrong.

"What happened?" Dex asked. Jason shook his head and walked to Madison. He picked her up and carried her to the house. We walked in the living and saw that Poppa laid the brothers side to side. Tyja was crying over JJ. Jason walked over and sat Madison down.

"How the fuck did this happen?" Dex asked.

"A fucking sniper." Jason mumbled. "Did anyone find him?" He asked. Tristan and Tank shook their heads.

"We went around the house and ran into some men. But we don't think that any of them was the sniper." Tank said. Jason's eyes landed on mine. I nodded. True to my word, I was about to deliver the sniper. We heard someone walk through the door. The shooter stepped in the room with the sniper rifle in his hand. Jason jumped up with the rest of the guys. Tyja saw him and looked over at me. Jason was ready to charge but I jumped in front of him.

"Wait!" I yelled. He looked down at me, breathing like a fucking bull.

"What?" He said.

"I asked if you trusted me. You told me yes. Know that I had to do this for you." I told him. He took a step back and grilled me. "Tyja got in touch with Ahmad before Matthews did. She set up a meeting and we talked. I told him that we didn't have anything to do with his brother's death. I showed him the surveillance that we had when his brother was working with them. He believed me and gave me information on Matthew's whereabouts. He wanted to kill Matthews but I promised him that you was going to do it. He told me that he would owe us anything. I asked for something that could put them to sleep so that they could stay out of the battle." I told him. Jason looked confused with everyone else. I looked back at Ahmad. "Can you wake them up please?" I asked him.

Ahmad dropped his weapon and pulled out a bottle of liquid. Jason was still skeptical. He move forward with Ahmad and that stopped him in his tracks. Ahmad looked at me nonchalantly. "In order for it to work, they will have to ingest it. I can't do that from here." He told him. I grabbed Jason's hand and I felt him tense up.

"Let him do this baby." I told him. Ahmad went around him and kneeled next Jo. Ahmad looked up at Jason.

"Do you want to help?" He asked him. Jason dropped my hand and walked over to Jo and JJ. Ahmad unscrewed the bottle and waited for Jason to open his mouth. He poured it down both their throats and pulled out a jar full with a pink paste. He put the paste over the wounds.

"That should do it." He said and stood up. "It was a good thing that you asked me to intervene. He had recruited Garnett. I took him out before he made a shot." He said. We heard Jo gasp for air and sit up quick. "He is going to need some water. They both will." He told us and picked up his weapon.

Tristan ran and got them some water. Jason was sitting in between them and waiting for JJ to wake up. He sat up and grabbed his chest.

"What the fuck?" He screeched out. Tyja wrapped her arms around his neck quick. "Damn it woman, let me breathe." JJ told her. She pulled back and kissed his face. Tristan handed them the water.

"What the hell happened?" Jo said weakly. He still looked drowsy from the drug that Ahmad shot in him. JJ looked up and saw Ahmad in the room.

"What the fuck is he doing here?" He asked. I stepped forward and explained everything to them. I didn't want them to be mad at Jason for something he had no control of. Jason relayed the message about a sniper having their eyes on them. Jo looked at me and smiled his understanding. She was happy that he did. JJ called me over and gave me a hug.

"Thanks for looking out for us, Girl. Even when we are being boneheads about it." He told me.

"No problem." I told him. Ahmad gave them some more pills and told them to take it daily for a week. He turned and looked back at Jason. "Whenever you need me, just call." He said and walked out of the door. Tank opened the floor and told the family that the coast was clear.

"Is anyone hurt to the point where they are about to die." T Glen asked.

"No Ma'am." Tank answered.

"Well, close it back up then. We good down here." She said. Everyone started laughing.

"What do you have down there?" Tank asked as he crawled his big ass down there. "Oh, shit. This is what I am talking about!" He yelled. That encouraged everyone else to go down there. Jo and JJ needed help getting down. Poppa's phone beeped and he frowned.

"What's wrong Poppa?"

"I got a message stating that the Elites weren't showing up because they were dead." He told me. My brothers and I opened up our phone to see if we got a message. We didn't which meant one thing. Eliria was hoping that Matthews killed us. She thought that we were dead and told everyone that we wasn't going to make it. "

Are they there now?" I asked Poppa. He nodded his head. I looked at my brothers and smirked.

"Are you guys ready to end this?" I asked them.

"More than. After this shit is over, I want Ahmad to hit me with the shit he hit JJ and Jo with. I want to sleep for a week." Kymel answered.

"You ain't never lying." Kymani said. They left the room to throw more clothes on. I turned and saw my babies and their father staring at me. I didn't know if he was mad at me or not. Sincere patched Madison up and gave her some Tylenol. I walked over to the children and gave them a big hug.

"Don't forget about the conversation that we need to have." I told them. They both nodded and went down to the room with everyone else. Jason grabbed my hand and stared down at me.

"Make it back to us. I'm sure you know that we have to have a conversation of our own." He told me.

"I know." I whispered. He placed his hand on my face and kissed my lips softly.

"Thank you." He told me. Kymel and Kymani came in the room with my bag.

"Let's go El." Kymel told me.

I pulled Jason down for another kiss. "I love you."

"I love you more." He said. I turned and walked to my brothers. Poppa was already in the driver's seat with the car running. Kymani hopped in the front while Kymel and I was in the back. I took my bag and pulled out my clothes to change. We rode in silence. It was the way we did things.

We got to an abandoned building with cars surrounding it. Poppa looked at us all and smiled. "Mi a proud poppa." He told us and held out his hand. Kymani dapped him off and then Kymel. I sat up and hugged him tightly. I pulled back and saw the fire in his eyes. "Nuh fuck round wid dem. Kill dem yah muthafuckas suh wi cya gwaan a vacation." He told us and that was the plan.

We jumped out the car and heard a crowd of people talking. We followed the voices and entered the building. It was more of a warehouse. A big ass open space with people sitting around, waiting for some action. Poppa cleared his throat. The voices died down and everyone's eyes landed on Poppa. Eliria's eyes got buck. She really thought that Matthews had a chance of killing us. She scanned our bodies and looked for injuries. The disappointment on her face was evident.

Poppa walked to the middle of the floor and pointed to us. "Di Elites ave arrive." He announced. The people in the room were shocked. Some of them were more than others because I did business with them. I used to babysit Mr. Alexis children for him when he went on missions. Kymel and Kymani were accountants to many in the room.

"Well, we see that you made it. Did you have any trouble?" Eliria fake ass said. I shook my head no.

"No, wi had cyar trouble." I answered. She smiled and walked to the middle of the warehouse with her brothers.

"Well who's first?" She asked. Kymani stepped forward and took off his jacket. He had his dreads up in a low ponytail.

"Di oldest." He said. The Hammer walked forward and removed his shirt. He had all types of hammers tattooed all over his body. That dude was big as fuck.

"Aye." I called out. "No fucking round." I told him. He walked back to me and kissed me on my nose.

"Neva," he said and dapped off Kymel. He turned back and walked to the middle where Hammer was standing. There were no bells or no sexy ass woman holding up a towel signaling us to start the fight. The fight starts with the first person that swings. Kymani looked for an angle and waited for the Hammer to act. Hammer went into fighting stance. Hammer swung a right jab and dropped his hand. That left his the right side of his face open for a hit. Kymani swung with a powerful left hook and dropped his ass flat on his face. Kymani stood over him, grabbed his head and snapped that bitch back. Kymel and I dropped our heads back.

"Shit." Kymel said. Kymani walked over to us, while looking down at his watch. "Three minutes." He said. He shook his head. "Get di fuck outta here." Kymani showed him his watch.

"Aight bet." Kymel told him and kissed me on my nose. He went to the middle of the warehouse. They already removed the Hammer's body from the floor. Eliria and her brother were staring at us with anger now. That was good.

Raine walked to the middle of the warehouse talking shit. "Vous allez mourir pour ce qu'a fait votre frère." Kymel laughed at him.

"Wah di fuck yuh tink did a guh happen?" Kymel asked him. Raine lost his cool and went at Kymel with wild punches, Kymel blocked them and hit that boy with an *IP Man* combo. It sounded like Kymel was beating on bongo drums. Raine fell to his knees in front of Kymel. Kymel roundhouse kicked Raine in the head. Raine stayed that way until his body fell to the side.

"Mmm," I moaned out. Kymani was shook up behind that one too. Kymel walked over to us.

"It a fi yuh tun sista. Mek wi proud." He told me. I was thankful for them. They finished them off quickly so that I can have all the time I wanted with Eliria. She was seething now. She didn't wait for me to come to the middle or for them to move her brother's body. She hopped over him and attacked me with a flying punch. I ducked and kicked her in the chest. She went flying across the warehouse. I didn't wait for her to get up. I told her that I wanted her to suffer. She jumped up and threw a right hook. I blocked it and hit her with a special hit. She gasped for air.

"Breathe." I told her and hit her with it again. "Breathe." I told her and repeated it twice. I punched her three times in the chest and watch the blood come out of her mouth. I spun and hit her in the forehead with a double elbow. She stumbled and tried to stay on her feet. I ran at her and watched her pull and throw two knives at me. I sidestepped one knife and caught the other. I threw the knife at her and hit her in the shoulder. She pulled it out and tried to throw it back. I dropped and rolled in front of her, with my blade in my hand. I swung my blade to her knees. I heard 'damns' and 'oh shits' around us. I heard Kymani and Kymel clapping and cheering me on.

Eliria yelled out in pain and fell down. She tried to crawl away. I strolled over to her and kicked her over. She looked up at me and was about to start talking. I didn't give her chance to. I slid my blade in her mouth and down her throat. She struggled and pulled at the blade. I pushed deeper, twisted it and pulled out. This feeling was something that I had never felt before. Freedom. I was free from to walk away from this shit if I wanted to. I am setting the platform for all the muthafuckers in this room. I left her with a huge hole in her mouth. I walked over to my brothers and looked around at all of the other killers in the room. I wanted them to take a good look at us and know that we are not for the games. Kymani had his phone out smiling and doing commentary. Poppa got up from his seat and walked to us without acknowledging the men that tried to talk to him.

"Mi ready fi dat vacation now." I told him. He nodded and led us out the warehouse.

Jason

We watched Joel kill Eliria on the big screen in the panic room. We knew that we couldn't sleep in the house, because of all the shooting that went on. We packed a few things and went to a hotel. We reserved the entire third floor for the family. I texted Joel and let her know where we were. I waited downstairs in the lobby for her. I knew that she was going to be tired. Shit we all were.

Callum pulled up and I walked out to meet her. As soon as she opened the door, I pulled her out and carried her to our room. We stayed in the hotel for a week. We ordered room service and watched more movies with the kids. It was the relaxation that we were looking for. We had our conversation about what she did to my brothers. At first I was pissed off with what she did, but I knew that she didn't mean any harm. She did what I couldn't do.

Callum went back to Jamaica with Reap and Shadow. Ever since the battle, people had been calling on them more and more. Especially with them taking out the Eliria's Gang. The Elites were now worldwide. Gage was getting orders left and right. But she was done with all that shit. She simply wanted to be Joel and I was fine with that. But she did finished off with one final job.

Abigail had been searching for Badrik for days. When she couldn't find him, she started packing and was trying to move out of Jamaica. When Abigail got in her car and placed her hand on the steering wheel, she felt a small pinched in her hand. She jumped and fell back in her seat.

"Ouch," she said and pulled her hand back to look at her finger. She placed her finger in her mouth and felt pain the moment her blood touch her tongue. Joel opened the backdoor to the car and watched Abigail struggle with the pain.

"I told you that, if you knew me, you wouldn't have crossed me. Now you will die the same way you paid that bitch to kill my mother, but only painfully. An associate of mine made this special type of poison for you, so you should feel special. It's a poison that inflects pain to your heart every time you breathe. I felt that you needed to feel what I had been feeling when I found my mother lying on the floor. I thought that I was going to die with every breath I took without her. Now you will die with no one knowing you or your stupid ass son. You have yourself to thank for that. Oh, well. Have a nice day." Joel told her and jumped out of the car. Abigail tried to reach for her phone to call for help. Badrik have caused so much turmoil in Jamaica that it tarnished the name that Abigail was trying to save. She sat there and cried until she couldn't hold on any longer. Abigail died ten minutes after that. Joel came back; she did what she could to help my brothers with their businesses. Kymel and Kymani became the family's Accountant. They gave us ways to save and make more money without dealing with outsiders.

Jordan was able to rebuild his car dealership. Lily and Jo decided to stay with Ma. She didn't want to be alone. She loved being around her grandkids. JJ and Tyja have their own spot in one of M&M apartment buildings. She stayed in Philly to help him rebuild his nightclub. Ma-ma been on their ass for grandchildren. Tyja tried to avoid the conversation. JJ winked at Ma and told her that he had a plan.

T Glen bought the house next door to Ma. She wanted their grandchildren to come up with each other. Tank and his girl, Alisa, have a two bedroom apartment in the same building that Tyja and JJ resided in. They were barely there because T Glen holds them hostage every time they went over there. Tristan is over the computer and security team over all of the Davis business with Dex.

Everybody was doing their own thing and living their lives. My brothers and I decided to take a trip down to New Orleans to visit Sincere. I invited Stipes down to announce some news. We were sitting around the table listening to the people sing on the stage at Sin's club. Tyja was singing and grinding all over JJ. That nigga looked like he was ready to go. Lily was checking her phone all night. Jo took the phone from her and put it in his pocket.

"Stop worrying about the damn kids. We are here to have a good time." He said and grabbed her hips. "Come here." He whispered and pulled her on top of him.

"Aye, where the drinks at?" Kymani said walking up the stairs.

"Mani," Joel stood up and hugged her brother. She hadn't seen them in weeks. They usually didn't go that long without seeing each other.

"Hey my Sis. What you been up to?" He asked her.

"She gotta be cooking because Jason getting fat as shit." Kymel said. Joel laughed and went to hug her brother.

"Fuck you, boy." I told him. He laughed and walked over to me. "You ready." Kymani asked me. Kymel looked at me and started laughing. "Don't back out now nigga. You look like you are about to throw up." I shook my head.

"Nah, I'm good." I told them. I looked at Sincere and nodded. He threw up a hand signal to the DJ. JJ and Jo looked at me and smiled.

"Alright People. We got a special surprise for you tonight. Here to perform his hit single. Ladies and gentlemen put your hands together for Daniel Caesar." The DJ announced. I watched Joel's eyes light up and went to the balcony that was over the stage. She started swaying to the melody with the girls.

Kingdoms have fallen, angels be calling
None of that could ever make me leave

I walked over to Joel and stood behind her. The guys came over and pulled their girls back. JJ almost had to put Tyja's goofy ass in a headlock. She was jumping up and down before I got down on one knee. I listened to this song every night when she left me the first. I listened to the words and knew that this was the song for us.

Ooh, who could've thought I'd get you
Ooh, who could've thought I'd get you

She looked to her left and didn't see me standing where she left me. She looked to her right to ask Tyja about me and saw that she wasn't there either. She turned all the way around and gasped. For the first time, she was caught off guard. She looked down at me and I let the song speak for itself. That was why it was perfect. She knew how terrible I was with words. She wasn't looking for no drawn out speech on why I wanted to marry her. She knew why because I showed her every day and was willing to do that shit for the rest of my life. When the song was over, I opened the ring box and showed her the ring that I got her. It was a Master Diamond Halo Band, with a three-carat princess stone in the middle. She didn't take her eyes off of mine though. She kept them on me and answered the question that was surrounding the moment.

"Yes, Jason. I will be your wife." She whispered. I took her hand and placed the ring on her finger. She pulled me up and pulled me into the most sensational kiss. I knew that her friends wanted to see the ring and talk about the engagement but I was ready to go. She must have felt the same way. Joel grabbed my hand and walked me to the stairs.

"I will see you guys later!" She yelled out over her shoulder. Sincere passed me my keys and dapped me off. We were outside in less than a minute. I opened the truck door and placed Joel in the passenger's seat. I kissed her softly and sung the chorus to the song to her. I didn't have a singing voice like Daniel, but she made me feel like I could do anything. That I can be anything. Her love has always been the key to my heart. And for that, I was grateful.

NOTE FROM AUTHOR

Note from Author

Thank you for reading *The Way to a Killer's Heart* series. I hope that you continue this journey with me as your Author. I have so many stories that I want to write and can't wait to share them with my readers. I will be continuing my paranormal series with Maxwell and Xoey's story from my first series, *It Took a Beast to Tame Her. I would love your feedback on this book and the chapter that awaits you. Enjoy and thanks again.*

MAXWELL

The Alph The King

Maxi

    I appeared in front of a house that looked like it was falling. Xoey was leaning on the light pole waiting for me to arrive. I was trying to get used to this teleporting shit. Xoey had been helping me with the Guardian magic that I possessed. I didn't know that I was Guardian 'til I was finished with my food in the woods. I didn't want to shift and run home because all the animals were trying to come through at once. I wished that I was back at the apartment and felt myself vanishing. I appeared in my apartment with the wild boar in my hand still. That shit was crazy. I told Xoey and she conducted some type of test to see how much Guardian I had in me. "Ma'vere must have been draining all of the Dark Guardians. They weren't powerful ones, but they had enough power to teleport and create illusions of the mind. You have to be careful of that. Sometimes you could fake yourself out to thinking that the illusions that you put out for other people, are real." Xoey told me. After that, I had been practicing every day.

I walked over to her and waited for her instructions. This was her mission, but I was ready to get to Nylah. "How are you trying to do this?" I asked her.

"We are going to knock on the front door and ask for her. Whatever happens after that, happens." She said looking down at her hand. Her blood ran black in her veins. I felt her changing. I didn't know if it was for the best or worst.

"Xoey," I called out to her. She looked up at me with red eyes. Her lips were parted and I was able to see her sharp teeth. She saw me staring and shook her head. Her eyes changed back to the grey that I was used to and the blood in her veins turned back to the original color. She walked passed me and towards the steps. "I am fine Unc." She said and dismissed anything else that was about to come out of my mouth.

"No, you are not fine. Have you told your mother and father how you have been feeling lately?" I asked her.

"No. Not yet. Mom is having a hard time with you not being there and trying to maintain a healthy pregnancy. Papa is trying to run the Southern Territory and stay on the board with the Elders. I don't want to be another problem." She replied. I grabbed her arm and swung her around to me.

"You are not a fucking problem. You are their daughter. They love you and would do anything to help you. You can't be around here feeling like something is taking over you and not tell the ones that you are around every day. They have the right to prepare for whatever is coming. Tell them or I will." I threatened. She sighed and nodded her head.

"If I tell Mom, she will feed me her energy and she needs it for Xaire. If she doesn't have the energy to use as a buffer for him, he will come out as a Darker Guardian. I have to try and figure this out myself." She said to me.

"But you are not alone, Xoey. After we take care of this and pick up Nylah, we will try to think of ways to keep you from going over. Okay." I responded. She placed her hand over my heart and patted it. That meant she agreed but had to think about how she was going to explain this to her parents. She turned and knocked on the door. We heard footsteps and someone unlocking the door. A woman head poked out and she looked us up and down.

"Who are you?" The woman asked. Xoey was not the one for the games. She stepped forward and smiled.

"You know who I am and what I am here for." She said softly. The woman eyes switch to mine. I flashed my wolf eyes at her and smiled with my wolf teeth. She slammed the door in our face and began to chant some shit through the door. Xoey shook her head and placed her hand on the door. It began to melt and dripped away. The women was standing in the foyer shocked at what she just witnessed. Xoey stepped in the house and looked around. "Where is Eve?" Xoey asked her.

"You can't have my sister!" The woman yelled and threw her arms out. The wall closed up where the front door was. The other doors in the room opened and big snakes came slithering out of them. I felt the animals in me stirring. I took a stepped forward to protect my niece. Xoey held her hand up and shook her head.

"No, Unc. Save your energy for the vampires. I got this." She said. Xoey walked forward and the snakes gravitated to her. She closed her eyes and exhaled. Xoey opened her eyes and hissed. She was now looking through snake eyes. She began to talk to them and with her tongue flipping like theirs. I have seen a lot of shit, but this was some cold ass shit. The snakes moved around and then stopped in front of her. They faced the woman and began to move her way. She backed up and tried to regain control over the snakes. The floors began to rock and the wall started shaking. I stepped aside and let whatever was coming through the now visible door. A giant cobra snake came busting through. Its eyes flashed on me and hissed. It circled around me in a comforting motioned and then moved towards Xoey. The other snakes wrapped themselves around the woman that called them out. She was trying to move but she was standing there looking like a burrito. The giant snake rose in front of her with its mouth opened. She yelled as the snake snatched her ass up and swallowed her and the other snakes. It turned around and greeted a smiling

Xoey. It leaned its head against hers and went back out the way it came in. Xoey looked back at me with her snake eyes fading.

"You are such a show off." I told her and walked forward.

"I thought that you would like that. I felt your dragon calling out to the snakes." She told me. I stopped and looked back at her.

"You can feel the dragon?" I asked her.

"I can feel them all." She said and walked pass me into another room. I looked down at my hands and saw that the dragon scales had popped up with my wolf claws out. I didn't know how I was supposed to get these muthafuckers to cooperate with each other, but something had to give. I followed Xoey in a room that looked rotten as shit. They had fruits on the table with maggots coming out of them and flies flying around the bowl that they were in. Xoey walked around the table. She tried to get a feel of the room. I felt that something was off but couldn't put my finger on it. There were six chairs at a round table. All the chairs was pushed in, but one. Xoey stood behind the chair and placed her hand on the back of it. She looked around the room and shook her head.

"This would have worked on a weaker Guardian, Lena. You know that. So, why would you waste me and my Uncle's time by playing these childish games?" Xoey said while looking in the corner behind her. She picked the chair up and threw it across the room. The chair hit the wall and something else made another sound hitting the floor. A woman appeared out of the corner and threw her hands out. She started chanting some shit. Xoey looked at the women, bored and unbothered. She walked over to where the thud sound came from.

"Leave my daughter alone, you demon!" Lena yelled. She looked as crazy as the snake woman. She was dressed in black rags with her hair all over her head. Her body looked like it was thawing out somehow. I didn't understand that 'til I saw the frozen snake on her forehead. I took a step forward and felt something grab my leg. I looked down and didn't see anything.

"Don't worry Unc. Eve is trying to find her way. Mimi took her eyes from her the day of the battle." Xoey said, while walking towards me. The woman was following behind Xoey chanting still. I didn't know what she was trying to do, but whatever it was she better try something quick before Xoey made her way over here. I guess her spell didn't work because she pulled out a knife and tried to stab Xoey in the back. I kicked an invisible Eve in the head, hopefully and vanished behind the crazy lady. She tried to turn towards me but I grabbed her by the back of her neck and lifted her up. Xoey held her hand over the spot where Eve crawled to. Her eyes shifted black and Eve body reappeared.

"Hello Eve. Why don't you have a seat?" Xoey said and placed her in the nearby chair. Lena started to struggle in my hand. I let my nails grew into her neck and placed my mouth by her ear. "Be fucking still or I will splatter you blood on these dirty ass walls." I growled. She stayed still and kept her eyes on her daughter. Eve sat in the seat with her head down. She had on the same rags as Lena and the woman in the foyer. I didn't understand their wardrobe. Xoey grabbed Eve's hair and pulled her head back. The place where Eve's eyes were supposed to be, was closed shut. "I need you to see death coming, Eve. You don't deserve an easy way out." She told her and waved her hand over her face. And just like that, Eve's eyes were back in place. Deep brown eyes were staring at Lena. Lena snuffles were heard throughout the room. I didn't feel sorry for her or Eve's bald headed ass. She fucked over my brother, Xavion. He deserved happiness with his mate.

"A woman with your beauty shouldn't have had a problem looking for love. Your obsession with my Uncle sentenced your family to death," she said pointing to the foyer. "And suffering," she pointed towards Lena. Xoey glared at Lena. "Come to me." Xoey said with her hand out.

"Nooooo!" Lena yelled but her voice got softer and softer until it was gone.

"Mother!" Eve screamed. She tried to get up. Xoey forced her to sit back down by moving her finger in a downward motion. She stood in front of her and squatted to meet her eye to eye.

"I will tell you what is about to happen to your mother. I will take all her senses away, including her ability to walk and talk." Xoey said and looked up at Lena. "I want you to see what will happen if you or anyone else in your family tries to come for mine again." Xoey told her and grabbed Eve face with force. I thought she snapped it. Xoey bonded Eve's body to the chair. She held her face up and made sure that Eve met her eyes. Xoey said something in a language that was not of this world. Eve started convulsion. She looked like she wanted to throw up. Xoey's eyes turned red and held her mouth open, over Eve's. Eve took in a deep breath and released it, along with her soul. It went up into Xoey's mouth. Eve's body slumped down in the chair with nothing bonding her to it. Her body hit the floor like a shriveled up prune. If Lena had a voice, she would have been screaming. Xoey looked back up at Lena with Eve's eyes and smiled. The shit freaked me out. I let Lena go and she landed on her feet. She took off towards Xoey. Xoey moved out of the way and Lena ran clean into the wall. When she tried to get up, she fell again and again. Xoey laughed out loud and walked over to me.

"I guess you are going to be needing a home healthcare provider. I know the perfect woman for that. She will also keep a close eye on you. Her name is Kimberly Smith. She will be here in a day or two." Xoey said in Eve's voice. Lena was beating on the floor with tears coming out of her blind eyes.

"Ready to go get Aunt Nylah, Unc?" Xoey asked me. I looked at her and shook my head.

"Remind me to not piss you off." I told her.

"You were close to it." She said. I looked back at her and waited for her to explain. "Every time I saw my mother crying for you, it did something to me. It made me angry. It will make her happy to see you. It will make them all happy. Just like you told me. You are not in this by yourself." She said. I hated when she used my words against me. We stepped over Lena and walked out the house.

"Aye, you don't think that taking in Eve's dark ass soul is going to add to whatever else is wrong with you?" I asked her. She shook her head no.

"Her soul don't have anything on the stuff that is inside of me. Eve's soul is the least of my worries." She answered and turned to me. "Grabbed my hand, so that I can guide you to the Covenant that

Nylah is in." She told me. I grabbed her hand and closed my eyes. I felt the wind picked up and knew that we were about to vanished. I opened my eyes and saw a black looking castle. We were standing at the front door. Xoey took a step back and gave me lead. I wasn't going to be pleasant and knock on the door. I warned Nyles and everybody else of what was going to happen if they tried to force her on anybody else. I raised my foot to kick the door down and my foot shifted into a bear's foot. The door went flying back.

"OMG Unc. That was a big foot." Xoey said behind me. I didn't have time to address her comment because the Covenant's guards were coming my way. I let my claws loose and ran to meet them halfway. The first guard swung and missed, which put him in front of Xoey. I knew that she was going to handle my lightweight. I swung on the second guard, opening up his throat with a swipe from my hand. I dodged the third guard and came up with an uppercut to the chin. His head went flying off his body. In midair, I kicked it towards the fourth guard's face. He stumble into the fifth guard, which had them falling on the floor. The sixth guard pulled out a sword. I stood in front of him and a lion's roar released from my throat. The sixth guard wasn't so sure about attacking any more. But I wasn't up for giving any of these muthafuckers mercy. I charged at him and bite his face off. He stabbed me with his sword while he struggled in my arms. I threw his body back with the sword stuck in my stomach. Strange thing about that was I didn't feel any pain. I pulled out the sword and threw it to the wall. The wound closed up right before everyone's eyes. The fourth and fifth guard stood up on their feet. They debated on who was going to attack me first. It didn't bother me none, because they both were going to die. They decided that they both were going to attack at the same time. The fire that spit out of my mouth torched them to the bone. I didn't know what type of fire that I had, but I knew it wasn't the regular fire that can be put out with water. I looked back to check on Xoey. Her face was covered in blood. I threw her a confused look.

"What the hell?" I asked her. She hunched her shoulders like she didn't know what I was talking about. I pointed to her face.

"Oh that." She said with surprise. "He ran into my mouth. It wasn't my fault. Honestly." She feigned innocent. I shook my head and went deeper into the castle. I didn't know where they were holding her. I tried to reach out to her but I couldn't get a scent on her. We traveled down a long dark hallway and came a split. I pointed in the other direction.

"Go that way Xo. If you see Nylah, reach out to me ASAP." I told her. She nodded her head and went left. I began to walk down the hallway with pictures on the wall. The first picture was of the Covenant when it was first built in 1765. In the picture, was of the family that was over the Covenant. Every picture after that was of the next generation that ran it. When I got to the last spot, there wasn't a picture. It had the gold plate labeled 2018 was placed below the picture frame. It wasn't going to be a picture either. I was going to take out the last descendant if he didn't stop fucking with me.

I got to the end of the hall and made a left. There were doors in this hallway, but the guards were guarding the door at the end. I closed my eyes and vanished. I appeared in front of the guards. Their reaction was too slow to stop what was about to happen to them. I took both of their heads and smashed it together until I heard the crunch that I was going for. I dropped their body and stepped closer to the door. I placed my hand to it and was zapped. It wasn't as strong as the one that Lil Bit used to shock me with. I looked down at the door handle and saw a hefty lock on it. The door was spell bound. I didn't think that none of the animals that were inside of me could take this door down. I was going to have use my Guardian to do this. Crazy thing about that was, I didn't know any spells to chant. I was about to call out to Xoey when I felt something familiar on the other side. I held my hand up and felt the blood in her veins calling out to me.

Enraged, I started punching and kicking the door. I didn't give a fuck if I was getting zapped. Nylah was in there and I had to get her out. I didn't know what they drugged her with, but her breathing was faint. I grabbed and held on to the lock.

"AHHHHH!" I yelled as I pulled the lock off the handle and

breaking the spell that was on the door. I rushed through it and saw that Nylah was strapped to the bed. I ran to her and ripped the straps of her body. They were also spell bound. The shit didn't hurt me as much, because of all of the power I possessed. But to Nylah, the shit could have killed her. I picked her up and started shaking her face.

"Nylah. Wake up, Baby. Come on and wake up for me." I told her softly. Nylah didn't budge. I grabbed her face and shook it some more. She still was unresponsive. She looked pale. I wanted to feed her but I didn't know what my blood would have done to her. I was ready to burn this muthafucker down, with everyone in it.

"Xoey, I have Nylah. She is unconscious and needs blood." I told Xoey. I walked back into the hallway and Xoey appeared in front of me. She placed her hand on her head and whispered something.

"She is lost in a place where there is no light. You have to talk to her Unc. Guide her back home. We can do that on the compound. Let's go." She said.

"No. You take her back to the compound. I gotta make sure that these bitches don't try nothing like this again." I told her and was handing Nylah to her. Xoey shook her head and side stepped me.

"Deniro isn't here. I searched this entire castle. We can't waist time waiting on him. Nylah needs help. Whoever put this spell on her, has made it to whereas if she doesn't make it out on time, she will be stuck in the dark forever. We gotta go." She said urgently this time. I looked down at Nylah's limp body. I was going to make these muthafuckers pay for real, for this shit. I nodded my head at Xoey. I thought of my room at my home, where my family were. I hoped that they were ready for the changes in me.

Coming June 30

COMING OUT SOON

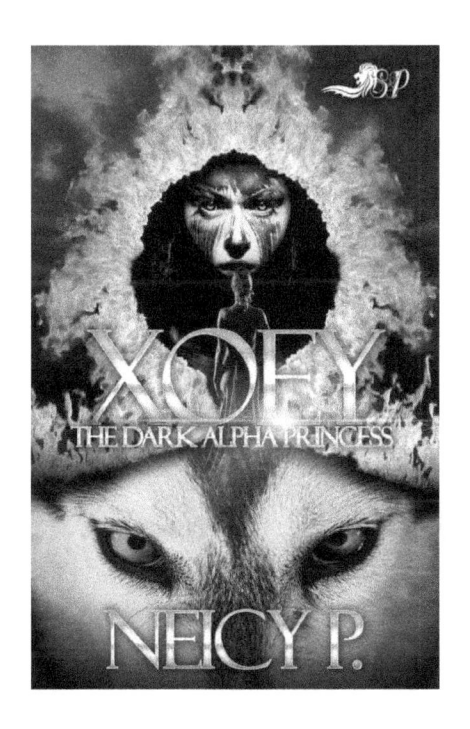

SUBSCRIBE

Text Shan to 22828 to stay up to date with new releases, sneak peeks, contest, and more...

WANT TO BE A PART OF SHAN PRESENTS?

To submit your manuscript to Shan Presents, please send the first three chapters and synopsis to submissions@shanpresents.com

CPSIA information can be obtained
at www.ICGtesting.com
Printed in the USA
LVHW081717271020
669965LV00010B/1355